Breaking the Rules

Meghann and I had just finished this great run to the bottom, when the lights flickered once, then went out, leaving the hill for a moment in darkness. There was a lot of grumbling, but people started gathering up their sleds.

"We have to go in," I said to Meghann. "Amy? Marcie?" I called.

"Wait!" Meghann grabbed my arm. "Why don't we try one more run down the hill, now that the lights are off? We could go out on the pond and into the woods and nobody'd know."

I looked at her. I had often thought of doing that once the lights were out. But I was always afraid Amy or somebody would see. Now, Amy was going on ahead with Marcie. . . .

We could do it. It wouldn't hurt anybody.

"No one would see us," Meghann said.

They might. "Nah," I said. "There are too many people around still. But I have an idea."

"What?" she said.

"Later," I said. "We could come out much later. After everybody is asleep."

Books by Patricia Hermes

Be Still My Heart
My Girl
My Girl 2

Available from ARCHWAY Paperbacks

The Cousins' Club: Everything Stinks
The Cousins' Club: I'll Pulverize You, William
Heads, I Win
I Hate Being Gifted
Kevin Corbett Eats Flies

Available from MINSTREL Books

The Cousins' Club

Everything Stinks

Patricia Hermes

A MINSTREL® BOOK

PUBLISHED BY POCKET BOOKS

New York   London   Toronto   Sydney   Tokyo   Singapore

This book is a work of fiction. Names, characters, places, and incidents are products of the author's imagination or are used fictitiously. Any resemblance to actual events or locales or persons, living or dead, is entirely coincidental.

A MINSTREL PAPERBACK *Original*

 A Minstrel Book published by
POCKET BOOKS, a division of Simon & Schuster Inc.
1230 Avenue of the Americas, New York, NY 10020

Copyright © 1995 by Patricia Hermes

All rights reserved, including the right to reproduce
this book or portions thereof in any form whatsoever.
For information address Pocket Books, 1230 Avenue
of the Americas, New York, NY 10020

ISBN: 0-671-87967-7

First Minstrel Books paperback printing February 1995

10 9 8 7 6 5 4 3 2 1

A MINSTREL BOOK and colophon are registered trademarks of
Simon & Schuster Inc.

Cover art by Chuck Pyle

Printed in the U.S.A.

For my friend Paula Danziger—
Happy fiftieth birthday

Everything Stinks

CHAPTER 1

I couldn't believe she'd be this unfair. How could she do this to me? My own mother?

I took a deep breath and looked across the kitchen at Amy, my twin. She seems to know, a whole lot better than me, how to get what she wants from Mom without a big battle.

Amy was looking at me now, shaking her head the tiniest bit, sending me a message. Amy is the nicest—and sometimes weirdest—person I know. And believe me, with our huge family of aunts and uncles and cousins, I know some truly weird people. But if they gave a prize for nice-but-weird, my twin sister would win it. She cares about people a lot, and she adores our little sister, Bitsy, like she's a mother herself. And when she and I fight—and we do that lots too—she's always the one who offers to make up first.

But the best thing about her—or worst, depending on how you look at it—is that she hardly ever gets upset with anything. I think a bomb could drop right here in the middle of the kitchen and she'd just go: I'll clean it up. I used to be like her when I was little, but not anymore. There's only one thing that seems to bother her, and that's if something happens to one of her old lizards.

But fighting with Mom over clothes? Amy couldn't care less. I think she'd have let Mom dress us like babies till we were forty.

Not me. I was going to try once more, even if Amy was signaling me to shush up.

"Okay, Mom," I said, much more quietly. "But why not? Just tell me that."

Mom sighed. She looked again at the catalogue I had just handed her, a catalogue with the coolest sweater in it I've ever seen, a sweater I wanted to buy with my own clothing allowance. "You know why not, Jennifer," Mom said. "It's not only expensive, it's all wrong for you. Heaven knows those baggy clothes you like are ridiculous enough. But this? Totally unsuitable. Unh-uh."

Bitsy, my little sister, repeated, "Unh-huh!" and I glared down at her. She made a face at me and then buried her head in Mom's lap. Mom rubbed Bitsy's back.

"But Mom!" I insisted. "I don't understand what's unsuitable about it."

"You don't?" Mom said. "Look at it!" She pointed to the sweater as if I had never seen it before. "Look how tight it is on the model. Lycra—and stretchy, for heaven's sake."

"You just said you don't approve of baggy clothes," I said.

Mom rubbed her forehead. "Don't confuse me," she said. "I feel bad enough with this cold."

"I'm not a baby anymore, Mom!" I said.

Mom smiled. "Once my baby, always my baby."

"Mom!" I glared at her.

"I'm your baby, right, Mom?" Bitsy piped up.

Bitsy is a baby, a four-year-old baby. And a big pain too.

"Now," Mom said to me, "why don't you and Amy get your homework done. That way, maybe after supper we can all play Scrabble or something."

"Wow, fun!" I muttered sarcastically. "Scrabble with the family."

"Jennifer!" Mom said, this warning sound in her voice.

I looked at Amy, who shrugged, and we both went up to our room.

"You should have waited," Amy said, as she collapsed on my bed and picked up a book. "Ask again later when she's in a better mood."

"Ha!" I said. "She'll never be in the right mood for that."

I flopped on my bed too, down at the bottom, and lay there, facedown.

Why were things always so rotten lately?

"Jennifer," Amy said suddenly. "Do lizards sing?"

Just what I needed: Amy to get weird right now.

I kept my head buried in the bed.

"Jennifer?" she said. She poked me in the back with her bare foot, hard. "Are you listening?"

"Now I am!" I said. I sat up.

"Sorry," she said, and she sat up too, then reached over and rubbed my back. "I didn't mean to kick so hard. But do you think lizards sing?"

"Sure," I said. "Just the other day, I heard one of yours going, 'la, dee, dah!' "

"I didn't mean like in 'la, dee, dah,' Jen, and you know it!" she said. "I meant like in humming sounds, musical sounds. You know how some creatures make their own music—not just birds, but dolphins, even. Do you think lizards do too, or maybe iguanas?"

I rolled my eyes at her. "Amy," I said, "lizards don't sing and they don't hum or make music either, okay? And neither do iguanas."

"I knew it!" Amy said. She held up the book she was reading: *Lizard Song/Iguana Music.* "They lied. I figured they did, because in all my pet books I've never heard of this."

"It's not a lie; it's just a title," I said. "Titles don't always have anything to do with the story."

Amy looked across the room to where she keeps her lizard cages. Yes: *Cages.* Plural.

4

"I thought maybe I could find a lizard that could sing and add him to my collection," she said. "Wouldn't that be neat?"

"Yeah," I said. "Can't you just picture your lizards waking us up in the middle of the night, singing their little heads off: Oh beautiful, for spacious skies . . ."

"Man!" Amy said. "You did have a bad day. Is it just the sweater?"

I shrugged.

No, it wasn't just the sweater. It was everything. Everything stinks. How come? Is it because the more you grow up, the worse things get? But it couldn't just be growing up, because Amy's my twin and she's not any different this year—unless it's because I'm the oldest, since I was born first, twenty minutes before her.

She was looking at me now with this worried kind of look.

Funny, but I already know what Amy's going to be when she grows up: a professional mother with about twelve kids, or a professional shrink.

"No, it's not just the sweater," I said slowly. "It's everything. Everything stinks! Mom tells me to act my age, and when I do, she gets weird. You heard her before: 'Once my baby, always my baby.' She'll never let me grow up!"

Amy just shrugged. "She was having a bad day. She has a cold, and Bitsy was being a pain."

"Bitsy's always a pain," I said. "And then how

about the cousins' visit? Last week Mom said Ed and Andy were coming over during winter break, and now they can't come."

"So?" Amy said. "Meghann and Mikie are coming instead, and you love them! And Meghann's the one who started the Cousins' Club."

"Right!" I said. "Like she'll ever let us forget it! Did you see the letter Aunt Alice sent, with the note from Meghann? 'Can't wait to see you! Remember, I'm president of the Cousins' Club.' Show-off!"

"So?" Amy said. "We'll have fun anyway. The Cousins' Club is always fun. And I love Aunt Alice and Uncle Vinnie."

Aunt Alice is Mom's sister, and she's married to Uncle Vinnie, Dad's brother—making our family all sort of double-related. Mom and Dad both come from really huge families. Mom has seven sisters, including Aunt Alice, and Dad has six brothers, including Uncle Vinnie—and they each have about a zillion kids. Every year, three or four times a year, one set of aunts and uncles and cousins visits another set of aunts and uncles and cousins. Sometimes we're the ones who visit, and other times we stay home and the relatives come to us.

The families are mostly nice, although there are some weird ones, like our cousin William, but we have the best times together. So one year we cousins began a club just for ourselves—the Cousins' Club. Actually, it was Meghann's idea, so she got to be president, and another cousin, Marcie, is vice president.

I shrugged now. I do like Meghann, in spite of her being such a big shot. But I'd been looking forward to seeing Edward.

"Anyway," I said, "that's just part of what stinks. At school I got in a big fight with Irma Ludinski over tryouts for cheerleaders. She's like, 'You can't try out, your grades aren't good enough.' And I'm like, 'It's only my spelling, and you should mind your own business.' And I called her a . . . name. Mrs. Colburn heard and I have to write an apology and Mrs. Colburn wants to see it tomorrow."

"Want me to write it for you?" Amy asked.

"Nah," I said. "Mrs. Colburn would know my handwriting."

Amy and I are in separate classes, because our school thinks twins do better if they're separated. Mom and Dad like it too, because they say we get to be more individual that way. As if we have to worry about that!

I sighed. "And then in the cafeteria, I accidentally bumped Irma . . . and it was accidentally. So her spaghetti spilled everywhere, and Irma started to cry, probably so she'd get sympathy and get a bigger serving, and she said I did it on purpose, and Mrs. Regular made me clean it all up! I was wearing my short jean skirt and I could hardly bend over, and the spaghetti was gross. It looked just like throw up."

Amy slid down on the bed, and opened her lizard book. But she kept looking at me, like she knew there was something else.

7

I looked away.

There was something else.

Boys. And those cheerleading tryouts. Because they're both sort of the same.

No, I don't mean I'm in love with boys, because I definitely am not, not the way some of the girls are. I can stand boys if I have to, especially if they're not into that stupid stage where they touch you and then go running away yelling things like "Cooties!"

But there's this one boy in my class who I like—not as a boyfriend, just as a friend, Robert Stagnaro. He's on the basketball team, so if I was a cheerleader ... Anyway, today I saw him staring at me, and when I asked what he was looking at, he said I had piano legs.

I didn't know whether to say thanks or make a face at him. I mean, I have the skinniest legs in the whole fifth grade. That's why I mostly wear jeans instead of skirts, except for today. But I always thought "piano legs" meant fat legs, so at lunchtime, after I cleaned up Irma's mess, I snuck off to the music room and looked at the legs of the big piano there to see if he meant my legs were getting fatter or more curvy or something. But piano legs are really straight and square, so I still can't tell if he meant it as a compliment or not.

I sighed. I hate boys. And spelling tests. And Mrs. Colburn. And fat old Irma Ludinski.

I started ticking things off on my fingers: And

straight legs. And piano legs. And show-off cousins. And fifth grade. And hair growing under my arms. And having to go to school on sunny days. And parents who dress you like a baby. . . .

"What are you doing?" Amy said.

"Counting off the things I hate," I said glumly.

"You're running out of fingers," she said.

"Amy?" I said, folding my hands behind my head. "You know Robert Stagnaro?"

"The one with the mole on his cheek?" she said.

I ignored that. "You think he's cute?" I asked.

"With the hair growing out of the mole?" she said.

"Amy!" I said.

"What?"

I refolded my arms across my eyes. "Forget it."

"What is it?" she said.

"Everything!" I said. "I told you: Everything stinks. I want . . ."

But I couldn't say what I wanted—at least I couldn't say it out loud. Because suddenly I thought I knew what I wanted, and it was going to be a long time before I was going to get it: I wanted to be in charge of my own life. If a day was good or bad, it would be because of what I had done—not because of what my mother let me do or didn't let me do, or what some stupid teacher said, or because of some ridiculous spelling test that could ruin my life. I wanted to be in charge of my own life. Then life wouldn't stink.

Now there was an idea.

I sat up and hugged my knees, looking at Amy. "If I had a plan," I said slowly, "would you help me with it?"

"Sure," she said. "I just told you I would. You mean, write the apology?"

"No," I said slowly. "Something else. I'll tell you when I figure it out."

I hadn't figured it out yet. But I would. I wanted to try it, try to have one day that I was totally in charge of. A day when I could be grown up.

Just one perfect day!

CHAPTER 2

I was still lying on my bed, thinking about a perfect day and about whether or not that would be ruined if I liked somebody who had a mole with hair growing out of it, when our bedroom door flew open and Bitsy came flying in.

She didn't knock and she didn't ask, just came running across the room, took a flying leap, and landed right on top of the bed. Also on top of both of us, her little legs pummeling me right in the middle of my chest—the second person to knock my breath away in the last hour.

"Bitsy!" I shouted when I could breathe again.

"Oops!" she said.

She backed away from me and closer to Amy.

Amy put both hands around Bitsy's waist, pulling her up onto her lap.

"What was that all about?" Amy said, burrowing her head into Bitsy's neck.

"I know a secret!" Bitsy said. "I know a secret. About Mommy and Daddy. And wait till you hear. But I don't know if I should tell you or not."

"What?"

Both Amy and I said the word *What?* together, and then Amy said, "Jinx!"

That's supposed to mean that I can't speak until Amy says I can—because we had both said the same word at the same time—but I wasn't in the mood to play a dumb game.

So I just said, "What's the secret, Bitsy? Tell us."

Amy glared at me, but I ignored her.

Bitsy always knows people's secrets. I think it's because she can be so quiet sometimes that hardly anybody knows she's around, and so people say things in front of her that they wouldn't say in front of anybody else. It's like she's totally invisible. Also, since she's only four, people don't think she understands. But she understands everything. I don't think even Mom and Dad realize how much she understands.

Bitsy's other big quality is that she's superdramatic. Like now. After bursting in here like that, she turned suddenly shy, lowering her eyes and fiddling around with a hole in the knee of her tights, a hole that was getting bigger by the minute as she picked at it.

I took her hand away from her tights. "Tell us,

Bitsy," I said. "And stop picking at that hole. You'll ruin your tights."

"I wasn't supposed to hear," Bitsy said.

"Well, you did," I said. "So tell."

Bitsy picked some more at the dangling threads in her tights, even though I was holding her hand.

"Come on, Bitsy," Amy said. "What did you hear? What are Mom and Dad going to do?"

Bitsy looked up. "Well," she said, in this whispery, dramatic voice that she puts on sometimes, "Mommy said she'd like to go away with Daddy all by themselves for a weekend. And Daddy put his arms around Mommy and he said he'd work it out. And then they saw me and laughed and called me a little rascal."

Bitsy giggled when she said that. For some reason, the words *little rascal* always make her laugh.

"So I don't get it," I said. "What's the big secret?"

Bitsy's eyes were shining. "Daddy said he'd call Mrs. Bedford," she said.

Amy and I looked at each other.

"Oh, no!"

Again, we said the exact same words at the exact same moment, but this time neither of us bothered to say "Jinx!"

Because Mrs. Bedford was a jinx enough. Bitsy loved Mrs. Bedford, but Amy and I were terrorized by her. Mrs. Bedford is always into some kind of food mode. Once it was a whole week of food that had no sugars and no salt. NONE. Another time it was just plain vegetarian. And once we had an entire week based on nothing but tofu. Tofu's a lot like toothpaste, only with no flavor. Also, Mrs. Bedford reads us Bible stories every night, all the way through dinner, concentrating on the goriest ones. And it's weird, but even though Bitsy is so little, she loves the gory stories, ones that make me sick to my stomach.

"But why not Mrs. Arnold?" Amy said. "I can't stand Mrs. Bedford! She won't let me bring my lizards out of my room—not even when I'm watching TV!"

"We had Mrs. Arnold last time," Bitsy said, "so it's my turn. Daddy said."

Bitsy was right: It was her turn. When Daddy gave Mom a rafting trip for her birthday last summer, we had Mrs. Arnold.

"This stinks," Amy said. "My lizards need a change of scene too!"

Bitsy shrugged. "But Mommy doesn't feel good. She wants to go away. She's got a cold!"

"When?" Amy interrupted. "Are they going before winter break?"

"What's winter break?" Bitsy asked.

I looked at Amy. I knew why she was asking. One time when Mrs. Bedford was due to come, Amy and I both pretended to be sick because we knew Mom and Dad wouldn't leave us then. It made me feel guilty to fake it like that, but I actually did feel sick just thinking about having Mrs. Bedford for an entire week. But then the weird thing is that I really DID get sick, Amy and me both. We got chicken pox. And I guess the truth is that I'd rather have Mrs. Bedford than chicken pox.

Anyway, I wondered if that's what Amy was thinking of—faking being sick when it was getting near time for Mom and Dad to go.

I sat up and looked at her. I'd fake it too. I'd do anything I had to.

"So go find out, okay?" Amy said to Bitsy.

"I'm not supposed to eavesdrop," Bitsy said. Very virtuous sounding.

"Then don't," I said. "Just ask. Or else just be yourself. Invisible. Sit on the kitchen floor and play with your Legos or Duplos. And then come back and tell us what you hear."

"Yeah," Amy said. "Pretend you're a secret spy."

Bitsy didn't say anything, but she slid down from the bed and began tiptoeing out of the room, her eyes shining again—a secret spy on a secret mission.

Honestly, that kid should be in the movies.

When Bitsy was gone, I looked at Amy and she looked back at me.

"We get sick?" I said.

Amy nodded. "But what if it's over winter break? We can't pretend to be sick on winter break or Mom'll make us stay in the whole time."

She slid off the bed, then went over to her lizard cage and brought back one of her lizards. She sat down on the edge of the bed, letting the creepy thing crawl up the front of her sweater while she gently stroked it with one finger. She had picked out one of the ugliest lizards—one with a kind of square red head that swivels practically all the way around.

I shuddered as I watched her. How could she like that ugly thing?

Both of us sat there, our ears strained, listening, Amy continuing to pet the lizard.

I could hear pots and pans being banged in the kitchen but not much else. Just a murmuring of voices.

Amy turned her head, watching her lizard, which had made its way all the way up her sweater, over her shoulder, and was now clinging head-down to her back. She reached over her shoulder, cradled it in her hand, then brought it up to her mouth and kissed it. Really!

I sat up. "I have an idea!" I said. "We're old enough to be sitters. Why can't we sit for ourselves? Why don't we see if they'll let us?"

Amy just shook her head. "You and I are old enough," she said. "Maybe. But what about Bitsy?"

"Right," I said, glum all over again. "But maybe they can take Bitsy with them?"

"Ha!" Amy said. "Some vacation that would be."

I nodded. I could just picture Mom and Dad trying to have a nice quiet dinner conversation in a restaurant. And Bitsy chattering nonstop, inviting strangers over to their table, commenting on the food—all of this in her super-loud, dramatic voice that she puts on as soon as she gets in a restaurant or store or something.

"Yeah," I said. "Bitsy would wreck it. No romance at all."

"Yeah," Amy said. She got up, went to the cage, and put the lizard back. As she came back and flopped onto the bed, she said, "I didn't mean to say anything bad about Robert before. It's just that I hate moles."

"Who cares?" I said. "I don't even like Robert."

And why had Amy thought of Robert when I was talking about Mom and Dad and romance?

I definitely do not feel romantic about Robert.

I was just about to say something about that when we heard Bitsy on the stairs. She hadn't closed our door when she ran out, so we could hear her clearly.

She came running down the hall, into our room, and was just about to make another flying leap at the bed—I could see how she poised herself at the door— but then she looked at me, quietly crossed the room, and climbed up onto the bed next to Amy, snuggling into her lap.

But her lip was out and her little face looked very sad.

"What's the matter?" I asked.

"Mrs. Bedford isn't coming," Bitsy said, her lip trembling.

"Yeah!" I said.

"Meanie!" Bitsy said, glaring at me.

"Mrs. Arnold?" Amy asked, hopefully.

"No. Nobody!" Bitsy said. "Just Aunt Alice and Uncle Vinnie. And I don't want them as babysitters. I want Mrs. Bedford."

"Aunt Alice?" I said.

"Uncle Vinnie?" Amy said.

Amy and I grinned at each other.

Aunt Alice and Uncle Vinnie! Meghann and Mikie's parents. If Mom and Dad went away while the cousins were here—wow! We could have the best time. Relatives never know—or else they don't care much—about the house rules and you can get away with murder, especially with Aunt Alice and Uncle Vinnie. They are just so cool.

"But I want Mrs. Bedford!" Bitsy said, and she looked so sad that I reached out and took her away from Amy and pulled her onto my lap.

"Bitsy," I said, "it will be okay. You know how much you like Mikie."

"I *like* Mikie!" she said. "I *want* Mrs. Bedford."

"I'll tell you what," I said. "You know how Mrs. Bedford reads you stories? How about while Mom and Dad are gone, I read you some stories? I know some good ones. New ones."

"Mrs. Bedford knows better ones," Bitsy said. But she sounded as though she might be persuaded to feel better.

"We'll get the very same book," Amy chimed in. "I'll read them to you too."

"The same book?" Bitsy said.

"The same book," I answered.

"At dinnertime?" Bitsy said.

I looked at Amy and she looked back.

We both shrugged.

Why not?

If it made her happier.

Because I was suddenly feeling happier. With Mom and Dad gone what could be better? I could do some of the grown-up things they never let me do—maybe even borrow some of Mom's clothes, the sexy ones. And the cousins would be here to make it even better.

Things were definitely looking up.

CHAPTER
3

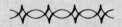

Either Bitsy had misunderstood what Mom and Dad said about a trip, or else Mom and Dad weren't being really honest with Amy and me. Because at dinner when we asked about them going away, Mom just shrugged and said, "Sometime. We haven't decided. A vacation would be awfully nice, but it costs money."

And Dad added, "Sometime soon. We hope."

"But Bitsy said you were going!" I said. "And that Aunt Alice would stay with us."

Mom just shook her head and leaned over toward Bitsy. "Little rascal!" Mom said, and Bitsy laughed.

Mom sat back. "All I said was that it would be a nice idea, a good plan if we could work it out." She frowned at me then. "You're not wearing lipstick, are you?"

I shook my head and bent over my plate. "Unh-uh," I said.

I wasn't . . . but I had bought a cherry chapstick. It made my lips kind of red and very shiny. Was Mom going to complain about *chapstick?*

Fortunately, Bitsy got her attention again.

"If you don't go when Aunt Alice is here," Bitsy said, "then I get Mrs. Bedford, right, Mommy?"

"If she's free, Bitsy," Mom said. *"When* we go, and we've made no decisions yet."

I looked across the table at Amy, but she wasn't looking back. She was busy dismantling this huge broccoli chunk that Mom insists on feeding us every night, cutting it with her fork into little bits. I knew what she'd do next: move the pieces all around her plate, making small piles here and there so it wouldn't look like she'd left it all. Which she would.

I had better plans for mine. I always smashed it down and buried it under one of the other things, like the mashed potatoes or the meat.

"But you've got a bad cold, Mom!" I said. "Some-place warm would be great for you! And you know with your artwork, your illustration work, you should keep warm. It keeps you . . . loosened up!"

Dad looked at me over his glasses—glasses he's just started wearing because he can't see to read the paper or, he says, even to see clearly what's on his plate. But when he looks far away, like across the table at me, then he can't look *through* the glasses but has to look over them. He's always frowning and adjusting them.

I'm never going to get old.

The frown he was giving me wasn't his these-glasses-are-making-me-crazy frown, though, but his "thinking" kind of frown. His head was tipped to one side, and he rested one finger in the cleft place in his chin. Dad is a college professor, and sometimes I think he deliberately tries to look the part.

"What?" I said, looking at him looking at me.

Dad just smiled. "Nothing," he said. "I'm just glad to see you so concerned with your mother's welfare."

I looked at Amy again, and this time she was looking back. I raised my eyebrows at her and she nodded a tiny nod, and then I nodded back. Our private signal. It means we're agreeing on something. It can be about practically anything, but this time it meant we both agreed to back off and not ask any more questions or anything. Sometimes with Mom and Dad, if we seem too anxious for something, they get very wary about it. And that would be especially true if they knew we were eager for them to go away.

Parents can be very suspicious.

But Mom and Dad did have some good news for us about the cousins. They were coming at the end of the week—Meghann and Mikie and Uncle Vinnie and Aunt Alice, and they were bringing another cousin, Marcie, who lives right next door to Meghann. Marcie's parents weren't coming because they didn't have any vacation time, but since Aunt Alice and Uncle Vinnie are both teachers, they had off the same week as we did. So we'd have Mikie, who's just four and Bitsy would love that; and then Amy and I would have Marcie and Meghann.

When we went to bed that night, I lay awake for a long time, thinking about the cousins and thinking about how to plan a really great day. What would be an absolutely fabulous day?

Getting new clothes, something grown-up and sophisticated looking, maybe something black if I couldn't get that Lycra sweater. Except that wouldn't work either, since Mom also says I can't wear black till I'm sixteen.

Not getting into trouble in school for one entire day.

Getting an *A* on the weekly spelling test and bringing up my grades so I could try out for cheerleader.

Having Robert Stagnaro notice me?

Well, not the way he noticed me today.

I sighed and turned over, staring out the window at the moonlit night. There was no way all those things could happen in one day! It sure wouldn't happen tomorrow, since I hadn't even studied the spelling words for this week.

But then I thought about winter break, when the cousins would be here.

What would make a great vacation day? Having anything I wanted for breakfast without worrying about Mom's "healthy" food, maybe something like leftover pizza or cold noodles. Or else there was a new box of Cap'n Crunch and Bitsy hadn't gotten the prize out of it yet.

Then when I went to get dressed, Mom would have bought me that sweater from Expressions, including the shiny black tights that went with it.

Ha! Like that would ever happen.

A new snow. We could go sledding. . . .

Nah, why waste a snow day on vacation? Better to have a snow day and have school canceled.

I know! Maybe Mom would say that Ed's parents had changed their minds and he was coming and then he'd see me in that new outfit . . . the one that Mom wouldn't let me get . . . and he'd think I looked so super and he'd ask me out.

Ask me out?

I actually said that right out loud.

Amy was asleep in her bed across the room, and she sat straight up.

"What?" she said. "Out where?"

But I could tell from her voice that she was still sound asleep.

"Go to sleep," I said.

"Sleep?" she muttered. But she lay back down.

Honestly, I thought, after Amy had quieted and lay back down on her pillow, I am such a jerk, an immature nerd. How could I want to be asked *out?* I don't even like boys. Besides, Ed is my cousin!

I sighed and turned over.

Was there something wrong with wanting boys to like you—if you hated them?

But there was a more worrisome thought still, and it was my twin: How come Amy didn't like boys or even notice them? Amy and I are different in a zillion ways—like I could care less about her stupid lizards, and she's organized and I'm not, and she's kind-hearted and I'm grumpy—but in the big things, we've always been alike. Mom says we both started walking on the very same day, and she says we said our first words on the very same day, and we're exactly the same size and we look so much alike that people can never tell us apart. Sometimes even Mom and Dad have trouble with that. We get sick at the same time with the same diseases, like that time with the chicken pox, and once we both broke our arms the same week, falling off the teeter-totter, and we both even got our first periods on the same day over last Christmas vacation.

Now Amy didn't care about guys. And I did. But I didn't.

I was afraid something was wrong with me.

Maybe I needed a shrink?

What do people do when they go to a psychiatrist? Do they talk about stuff like this? Or does the doctor look at you and he can tell exactly what you're thinking and you don't have to say anything?

That would be good. But bad too. What if you don't want him to know what you're thinking?

Or what if *he* is a *she?*

Maybe I could talk better to a she. At least she'd

understand—maybe—how you could hate guys but want them to like you at the same time.

I turned over again but couldn't get comfortable. I punched my pillow into shape, pulled the quilt up around my ears.

My two bears, Big Bear and Little Bear, that I've had since I was a baby and that I always used to take to bed were both now on my nightstand.

I looked across the room to Amy's bed, wondering if she was really asleep, then quietly slid both Big and Little into bed with me.

I snuggled Big under my arm and Little under my pillow, just the way I used to do. I always rubbed the red ribbon around Big's neck too when I was a baby, then sucked on my pacifier—my puffer, I called it.

I didn't really want a puffer now, but the bears did feel good.

I was just drifting off to sleep, rubbing Big Bear's old, soft ribbon, when suddenly I was wide awake. The written apology to Irma! I had to hand it to Mrs. Colburn tomorrow.

It was so embarrassing to have to do that! Besides, how could I say I was sorry when I wasn't? And what could I say that would satisfy Mrs. Colburn but wouldn't satisfy Irma? I was sure Irma would show it to all her friends.

I pulled the covers tight around my head. I'd write it in the morning.

But I still had to study my spelling words for morning. I'd never get it all done.

Why wasn't I organized like Amy?

Maybe I'd pretend to be sick and stay home.

Nah, not with winter break coming up. Like Amy said, Mom would keep me in the house the whole week, believing I had a cold.

I sighed and sat up, pulling the quilt around my shoulders and tucking Big and Little under my covers.

On my bedside table, I have this tiny book light that Amy gave me for our birthday once, because I love to read in bed but the table lamp keeps her awake.

I switched on the book light, then got a pad of paper and pencil.

I propped my pillow up against the headboard, then leaned back against it, the pad of paper resting on my knees, and picked up the pencil.

"Dear Irma," I wrote.

I chewed on the pencil. Dear Irma *What?*

Maybe it should be her full name, Irma Ludinski.

I bet she hates her full name. I know I would.

"Dear Irma Ludinski," I wrote. "I am sorry . . ."

Well, I'm not really sorry about anything. But I had to say so, since that's what a written apology is.

I thought some more and then came up with this:

Dear Irma Ludinski,

   I am sorry that you did not mind your own business about my grades. And I am sorry for calling you a name. Even if Thunder Thighs is a good one for you. I will not call you names again. As long as you do not interfere anymore.

Anymore? Or was it *any more?*—two words? Did you have to check spelling for an apology?

I reread the letter.

It was pretty good, but for that part about thunder thighs.

That was kind of mean.

If I were Amy I'd take it out.

I sighed. I erased the part that said "I am sorry for calling you a name. Although Thunder Thighs is a good one." And I wrote instead "I am sorry for calling you Thunder Thighs." That way I got to say it again, but I wouldn't feel too bad about it. Also, Mrs. Colburn wouldn't get mad this way.

There was so much erasing that the paper was thin, but it would just have to do.

I put the letter on my table, turned out the light, and settled down with Big and Little again, feeling good that I had gotten this over with.

Tomorrow sure wouldn't be that great, not with having to give that letter. But I now had time to study for the spelling test in the morning, and with winter vacation coming—and the cousins—maybe life wouldn't be so rotten anymore.

CHAPTER
4

If you can't say something nice, don't say anything at all.

That's what Mom used to say to Amy and me when we were little and were having a fight. Of course, Amy and I made up our own saying: If you can't say something nice, *whisper* it.

We whispered lots of not-nice things to each other.

But now it was Friday night. This miserable week was behind me. And all I could think of was Mom's saying: Don't say anything if you can't say something nice!

Well, what if there's nothing nice about your whole life? Would you have to become one of those monks or nuns who don't speak at all? That would be me, because there was surely nothing good to say about this past week and today especially: Mrs. Colburn didn't like my letter at all, and I had to write an essay on "friendship" over winter break. Irma hated the letter too and burst into tears when she read it, and for some weird reason that made me feel bad. (But still happy because she couldn't show it around to her friends because of my writing Thunder Thighs there.) Also, I failed the spelling test, even though Amy quizzed me on the words all the way to school. And at school all day, I wore the baggiest jeans I own and sat with my legs folded up under me so Robert Stagnaro wouldn't notice they looked like piano legs, and I got pins and needles, and when I got up and stamped my feet, Mrs. Colburn got mad at me. Again. And just last night, I had thought life might not be so bad after all. Ha!

Anyway, it was Friday night. The start of winter break. The cousins were coming sometime after dinner. Later in the week, Mom and Dad might go away for a few days. And I was going to forget about school for an entire week.

After dinner, since the cousins hadn't arrived yet, Amy and I went outside with our sleds in the snow, even though it was dark. We live on a big hill, right next door to a big white church with a steeple on top. The church is pretty, especially at night in the snow, and the church people always keep a big floodlight on, lighting up the front of the church and the hill and the little pond at the foot of the hill. That means there's plenty of light to sled by, and all the kids in the neighborhood sled there until the light goes out at nine o'clock. The neighborhood parents and the church people have all sorts of rules about us playing there. The biggest rule is that we must never, never, never go out on the pond, even if it looks frozen. It's a small pond, but it's very deep. And we can't litter, and we can't use bad language, and when spring comes, we all get together and help rake the lawn and plant grass seed and make the hill pretty again. But as long as we keep to all those rules, then we're allowed to sled on the church hill.

Now Amy and I were just piling onto our sleds, ready for a race, when we saw a car pulling into our driveway next door: The cousins had come!

We grabbed up our sleds and ran home, just as the car door was opening, and Marcie and Meghann and Mikie piled out, Mikie holding that train case of Legos that he carries with him everywhere.

"Hi Meghann, hi Marcie," I called.

"Hi Mikie!" Amy said, hugging Mikie to her.

Meghann and Marcie were standing just by the car door, hugging their arms to themselves and dancing up and down in the snow, trying to keep their feet warm.

We live in Connecticut and they live in the southern part of Virginia, and they weren't dressed for snow.

"We didn't know it had snowed here!" Meghann said. "I didn't even bring boots."

"Me neither!" Marcie said.

"Don't worry," I said. "Amy and I have plenty. You can borrow some. Come on! You want to sled now?"

They both said yes, but before we could head for the house to get them the right clothes, Mom and Dad arrived outside, and Bitsy too. Everybody was milling around in the driveway, saying hi to everybody else, and the grown-ups were saying things like "My, how you've grown!" And all that stuff.

Amy and I said hi to Aunt Alice and Uncle Vinnie, and Uncle Vinnie gave Amy a big bear hug. "Hi ya, Gorgeous!" he said.

Then when he hugged me, he said, "Beautiful!" He held me away and looked at me. "Even more beautiful than last time."

I made a face at him, but secretly I loved it. I was glad I had put on more cherry chapstick.

Then Amy and I went into the house, Marcie and Meghann following.

Once upstairs in our room, Amy started showing Meghann and Marcie all the new stuff she'd gotten since we saw them last—her computer, the little box on the night table where she keeps her treasures, all her Christmas stuff.

While she did that, I just watched, trying not to be obvious, but studying my cousins all the same, trying to see if they had changed or grown up or anything since I'd seen them last.

Meghann was wearing a blue sweater and jeans, and

she had pulled her hair up in a ponytail at the side of her head. It made her look a little lopsided, but kind of cool. And the sweater brought out the blue in her eyes. She really has awfully pretty eyes, a deep blue with sparkles in them. She also has a tiny, heart-shaped face and really pale skin, but it's totally smooth, and she doesn't have any freckles. Or zits.

I glanced again at the front of her sweater.

Flat. Just like me.

I looked at Marcie then. She looks a lot like Megh-ann, almost enough for them to be sisters, even though they're just cousins. The only difference is that Marcie wears glasses and Meghann doesn't. And actually Marcie is a little prettier than Meghann—yet Meghann looks more mature or something. Now Marcie was dressed just like Meghann, so they actually almost looked like another set of twins—except that Amy and I never dress alike.

It was really good to see them. I like them both a lot, even if Meghann is sort of bossy.

I bent down and began rummaging in my closet, pulling out old boots and sweaters and a pair of ski pants. I held up the ski pants. Man! I had almost forgotten those. What an awful weird color—olive green with orange trim!

Ugly, but they'd be warm.

"Here!" I said, holding them out to Marcie, but Meghann grabbed them first.

"Brat!" Marcie said, shoving Meghann with her shoulder.

Meghann just laughed.

Marcie made a face at her, but by then Amy was digging in her closet and had come up with some stuff, and she handed a pair of pants to Marcie.

It took a few minutes, but soon we were all dressed in weird old stuff I had half forgotten: a purple snow jacket that was really short in the sleeves for Meghann and a red one with fur on it for Marcie, boots and ski pants for them both, along with a couple of woolen ski hats with tassles on them that someone had given Amy and me once but that were too ugly to wear except in emergencies like now. We couldn't find matching mittens, but we did find enough odd ones to make two pairs.

I had taken off my ski jacket and mittens while I dug stuff out, and I began putting them back on while the others dressed.

"Know what, Jennifer?" Meghann said as she tugged on ski pants. "We have a project for winter break. I thought of you right away."

"I hope it's an essay on friendship," I said. "You write it; I'll use it."

"How come?" she asked.

"Nothing," I said. "I'll tell you about it later. What's your project?"

"To bring in something we used to love when we were little," Meghann said.

"So why did you think of me?" I asked.

"Because of Big Bear and Little Bear, silly!" Meghann said, laughing. "You always bring them with you."

"Not last time I didn't!" I said. I glared at her.

She shrugged. "You used to," she said.

"When I was a baby!" I said.

I turned away from her. What a pain!

"Ready, everybody?" I said when I was finished getting my things on. "We'll have to share sleds because we only have two."

"I call Jennifer!" Meghann said.

I wondered if that was her way of making up.

We went downstairs and outside, then raced next door to the church hill.

It was still crowded with people, especially because everyone was at the start of winter break.

I sat down on the sled, my feet on the steering bar, and Meghann climbed on behind me.

Amy and Marcie gave us a running start, and we zipped off down the hill.

Just before the bottom, down by the pond, I tipped the sled to the side, the way we always do—the only way to keep from sliding out onto the pond and across it and out into the woods—and it dumped us both into the snow. I needed to do it to stop, but it also felt good, like getting back at Meghann just a little.

Meghann came up laughing, but then she asked, "Why did you stop us?"

I brushed the snow off my pants and grabbed the sled rope and started back up the hill. "It's the only way to keep from going out on the pond," I said.

"So why don't you go out on the pond?" Meghann asked.

"It's a rule," I said. "A parents' rule."

"But why?"

I shrugged. "Because once a thousand years ago some kid crashed through the ice and almost drowned."

"It looks frozen solid now," Meghann said.

"It is frozen," I said. "It's been frozen since Thanksgiving. I always want to do it because once you get past the pond, you can go forever on the other side in the woods. There's even more hills over there."

"Then why don't we try it?"

"We'd get in big trouble," I said. "Somebody would tell. One of the boys, Arthur Lamb, did it last year and the pastor heard about it, and every kid in the neighborhood was banned from the hill for a whole month. And we had practically a blizzard that very same week but we couldn't sled and nobody spoke to Arthur Lamb for the rest of the winter."

We were at the top of the hill again, and for this ride down, we decided to belly flop. I lay flat on the sled, and Meghann lay on top of me. With our arms and hands, we pushed ourselves in the snow till we got us going fast, then zipped our way down the hill.

This time when we got to the bottom, we were going slow enough that we didn't have to tip over into the snowbank.

Meghann got up and took a few steps out onto the ice.

"It's really solid," she said.

I nodded and waited for her to come back in.

She did, and again we started back up the hill.

We slid a bunch more times. Sometimes I took turns with Marcie and sometimes with Meghann. Meghann and I had just finished this great run to the bottom when the lights flickered once, then went out, leaving the hill for a moment in total darkness.

There was a lot of yelling and booing, but people began gathering up the sleds. Then as my eyes got accustomed to the dark, I could see that it wasn't really pitch dark at all, that there was a big moon and the stars hung low—a beautiful night.

"We have to go in," I said to Meghann. "Amy? Marcie?" I called.

"Wait!" Meghann grabbed my arm. "Why don't we try one more slide down the hill now—now that the lights are out? We could go out onto the pond and into the woods and nobody'd know."

I looked at her. I had often thought of doing that once the lights were out. But I was always afraid Amy or somebody would see. Now Amy was going on ahead with Marcie. . . .

We could do it. It wouldn't hurt anybody.

"No one would see us," Meghann said.

They might. I shook my head. "Nah," I said. "There are too many people around still. But I have an idea."

"What?" she said.

"Later," I said. "We could come out much later. After everybody is asleep. No one would be here to see us then."

"Could we?" Meghann said. "Really?"

I nodded. "Yup. But we better not tell Amy. She worries."

"Okay," Meghann said. "Hey, remember that summer when we went out on the roof at my house one night and stayed up to watch the sun come up?"

"Yeah!" I said. "But listen, what about Marcie? Should we let her come with us later?"

Meghann didn't answer for a moment, and then she said, "There's only two sleds?"

"Right," I said. "There's only two sleds. Okay, so we don't tell her."

"Is it easy to sneak out of your house?" Meghann asked. "Will your parents hear?"

"Nope," I said. "With that back stairs, Amy and I get in and out easy."

"Have you ever done this before?" Meghann asked.

"Other stuff," I said. "Never this."

"But they'll never know," Meghann said.

Both of us were quiet then as I grabbed the sled rope and we headed back up the hill to the house.

Ahead of us, we could see Amy and Marcie trudging along, their sled dragging behind them.

"Besides," Meghann added, kind of serious sounding, as if she was having an argument with me—or herself—"rules are made to be broken, right?"

I didn't answer.

They were. And this was a dumb rule. The pond had been frozen for months. But secretly I was more than just a little worried: What if this rule was a good one? What if my parents were right about this one?

CHAPTER
5

I thought Amy and Marcie would *never* stop talking and get to sleep. Meghann and I both pretended to be too tired to talk, hoping that would make them shut up. But no. On and on they went, talking about everything from school to lizards to lizards to lizards. I was struggling to stay awake, and I kept poking Meghann, who was sharing my bed, to be sure she stayed awake too.

Eventually, both Amy and Marcie fell asleep. First there were longer and longer periods between what they said, and then I could hear Amy's breath coming heavy and slow and deep, and then Marcie actually began snoring!

Both Meghann and I crept out of bed and dressed silently in the dark.

It was very late and very silent when we finally got out into the freezing, cold night. It was also dark. If I said that about the dark to Amy she'd tell me that by definition nights are dark, but this was darker than most. At least it felt that way. The moon kept hiding behind clouds, and the clouds themselves were much thicker than they had been at nine o'clock when the church lights went out. I couldn't even see the pond at the foot of the hill and I could hardly see Megh-ann's face right next to me.

During that whole time that Marcie and Amy had been talking, I had lain awake staring at the ceiling, worrying, and now that we were out here on the hill, I was still worried. It's not that I'm a chicken or any-thing. And it really wasn't that I was afraid of falling through the ice. In fact lots of times kids walk out on the pond, just run out and then back, like daring themselves. Or daring the grown-ups to see them. But taking a sled out there was different, as Mom and Dad kept telling us. The weight of the sled, distributed on just those two narrow runners, with the weight of a person on it—well, according to them we could crash through and get trapped under the ice and die. But even that wasn't what was worrying me, because I didn't think for a minute that the ice would break. I mean, the temperature hadn't gotten above freezing since Thanksgiving.

I was worrying more about something else and it was this: Our family sort of has a rule—one about trust. Mom and Dad say that the whole world really works on trust. For example, Mom and Dad say they trust us not to do things we shouldn't do, and they trust us to do the things we should. And in turn, we trust them to do the things they are supposed to do—like care for us, make a living for us, teach us. At least once a week, at dinner, we have this big conversation about trust. And now it was worrying me.

See, it's not that I never do anything I'm not supposed to do. Because I do, and Amy does too, and Bitsy *always* does. But this thing about the ice seemed like an important part of trust, maybe because Mom and Dad said it was so dangerous.

But I kept telling myself, the thing is, it *wasn't* dangerous.

"It's really not dangerous."

I turned and looked at Meghann.

We were standing at the top of the hill, looking down, each of us holding a sled by the rope. And she's the one who said that, like she was reading my mind.

"I know," I said.

"Even if it was dangerous, we're doing it, right?" she said. "I mean, it's not *that* dangerous."

"It's not," I said. "Ready?"

"You?" she said.

I wasn't.

I looked down the hill to where the pond must have been—although I sure couldn't see it from here.

"Yup," I said.

"Did someone really almost drown there?" Meghann said.

"Mom says they did. But I was just a little kid. I don't remember. Come on. Let's do it."

I dragged my sled to the best place at the top of the hill, the one where there's a straight, long, steep slide down, without any bumps. When the older kids are here, especially the boys, it's impossible to get near this good spot.

I stood there with my sled, and Meghann stood right next to me.

"What if someone sees us?" Meghann whispered.

"Who can see us?" I said. "*I* can hardly see you."

She giggled. "Good thing. I look like a nerd in this hat."

"Ready?" I said.

"Yup," she said.

I held my sled in front of me, up against my chest. Then I began to run. I took some quick, really quick running steps, then flung myself down on my stomach on the sled—bellyflopping, it's called.

Next to me I could hear Meghann doing the same thing.

She made a big "Whoompf!" sound when she came down on her stomach.

Side by side, we went racing down the hill.

The night air rushed by, and for the first time since we had decided to do this, I felt good about it.

It was just so neat being out there in the dark, just us.

The foot of the hill was rushing up toward me.

Yes.

The foot of the hill. The bottom.

And I was still going. Fast.

Did I dare keep going?

I held my breath. And closed my eyes.

Do it!

For the first time in my whole entire life, I didn't do anything to slow myself down.

A little bump and then a thump as I dropped a few inches and down onto the pond.

And then, like lightning, I was speeding across the pond.

Another little thumpy sound—Meghann's sled dropping down onto the pond behind me.

Then Meghann yelling, "I love it!"

And we were across the icy pond and out the other side and into the woods. There's just a tiny rise there, but we were going so fast that we kept right on going up, and then were heading down the next hill. Fast.

But here it got really scary.

That side is hard to get to if you don't go across the pond, so we don't do it much and I don't know the hill like I know my side. Also, without the moon, it was hard to see.

But it was as if my sled had eyes—or at least a mind of its own.

I went crashing down the hill, snow flying everywhere.

I must have been going thirty miles an hour—or at least it felt like that. Snow flew up as I steered around trees and tree stumps. Sometimes, though, the trees appeared so fast it was hard to steer, but somehow I managed to avoid them all.

And then behind me, I heard this *THUMP!*

And Meghann yelled again.

This time she wasn't just excited. She was hurt. Or scared. Or something.

God, don't let her have run into a tree.

I dragged the toes of my boots to slow myself, then rolled off the sled and looked back.

"Jennifer!" she called. "Jen!"

"What?" I called.

"I got hurt!" she said. She sounded as if she was crying.

Oh, man! Trouble.

"I'm coming!" I said.

I picked up my sled, then climbed back up the hill to her, slipping and sliding all the way. She and the sled and all were dumped over in the snow.

She was sitting up, holding her head. But at least she was sitting up.

"What happened?" I said, kneeling down next to her in the snow.

"I think I ran into a tree," she said, in this small, whimpery voice.

"You *think* you did?" I said.

"Uh-huh," she said, holding both hands to her head now.

I don't think I've ever seen Meghann cry, but she was sure near tears then.

"I know," I said. "We were going so fast. It's your head?"

She nodded. "Can you die of a fractured skull?" she asked, her voice quavering.

"You don't have a fractured skull," I answered.

"How do you know?" she said, not looking up at me.

"Because you're . . . talking," I said.

I didn't know if that was true, but it sounded right. I mean, if people fracture their skulls, they get unconscious, don't they?

"It feels like it's broken," she said. And then she did begin to cry. "Oh, Jennifer!" she said. "Last summer William said that he heard about someone who got a fractured skull, but when it healed some of their brain was left on the outside of their skull. Do you think that's true?"

"You know it's not true!" I said. "Our cousin William is too weird for anything, and you know it. Now give me your hand. Can you stand up?"

She nodded, but when she did, she winced. But she wiped her tears with the back of her mitten and held out her hand, and I pulled her to her feet.

When she was standing up next to me, I looked at her closely.

The moon had come out again, not bright, but just with this kind of wispy look, a thin circle of light around the moon.

It was enough light to see by, though. And to see that there was blood on Meghann's face. And blood on her mittens.

"Uh-oh," I said.

"What?" she said, and her voice started rising. "I knew it! You can see my brains, right? Oh, William was right, wasn't he?"

"Meghann!" I said. "Stop it. Hush up! You want somebody to hear? And no, I can't see your brains!"

"You can too!" she said.

"I cannot!" I said. "Besides," I added, trying to make her laugh, "you probably don't have any brains. But I do see blood."

She looked down at her mittens.

There was blood all right.

"How bad is it?" she asked.

"Let me see," I said, bending in closer to her.

"If there's brains, don't touch them!" she said.

I just shook my head, then pushed her hat and hair away from her forehead, peering close.

There was a big line of blood just above her eyebrow, right above her right eye. But that was all I could see. That and a bump.

"Not big. Just a little cut," I said. "Is this where it hurts?"

Carefully, I touched the spot above her eye.

She nodded. "There. Are you sure there's no brains?"

I didn't even answer that. "Does it hurt a lot?" I asked.

She took a big, shuddering breath. "Not that much. Not as much as when I broke my arm last summer. But what if it needs stitches?"

"It won't," I said.

I hoped.

"Jennifer?" Meghann said. "Do you think we shouldn't have come out here?"

"Nobody ever said we shouldn't slide down this hill," I said. "All they said was don't go out on the pond. And we didn't get hurt on the pond."

For some reason her question made me angry. Maybe because I knew we shouldn't have been out there.

But until she hit the tree, it had been a lot of fun.

Meghann took another deep, shuddering breath. Then she bent down, scooped up some snow in her mittened hand, and held it to her forehead.

"I'm going to wash it off this way," she said. "Help me. But don't hurt!"

Gingerly, I helped her wipe the blood away with the handful of snow.

It really wasn't a very big cut—maybe an inch long and not real wide. But as we wiped away blood, more blood crept up, making a thin red line above her eye that kept filling up with red every time we wiped it clean.

"How does it feel?" I asked.

"It hurts," she said.

She patted around her eye and her forehead with

both hands, like she hadn't really believed me about the brains thing. "Promise something?" she said.

"What?" I asked.

"Just promise," she said.

"Okay," I said. "I promise. What?"

"Promise you won't tell anybody what I said about my brains coming out of my cut."

"I won't tell," I said.

She sighed. "I laughed at William when he told me that last summer," she said. "But it scared me anyway."

"Let's go home," I said. "And I'd be scared too if I ran into a tree."

We both picked up our sleds and headed for home, Meghann wiping the blood away from her eye every so often.

When we got back to the pond we walked straight across it, not even stopping or worrying.

After all, it had held our weight the first time.

Quietly, we climbed the hill toward the house. We left our sleds on the back porch and snuck up the back stairs to our room.

No one—not even Thomas, our cat—seemed to be stirring.

As we took off our things and crept into bed, I had this funny thought. I thought I knew one thing that was wrong with being a grown-up. See, maybe parents *do* know certain things. But then, because they know a few things, they get cocky and think they know everything. I mean, maybe it was not a *good* idea to go sledding in strange woods in the dark. But maybe it wasn't a *bad* idea to sled on a pond that had been frozen since Thanksgiving.

I'd have to think about that. About rules. But for right that moment, the only thing I was thinking about was sleep.

Sleep, which didn't come all that quickly as I worried about what would happen when our parents saw Meghann's forehead the next morning.

CHAPTER
6

Next morning two things happened—one good, one not so good. The good was that Meghann's cut had stopped bleeding and was easy to hide under her bangs. The bad was that she had a black eye. Well, not exactly black—why do people call black eyes "black"? Actually, they're sort of blue and purple, which is what Meghann's was that morning. A deep, shiny purple. And there was no way to hide *that* under her bangs!

We did try with makeup, though. I snuck into Mom's room and used some of that concealer she uses to cover blemishes and stuff. But it didn't do anything but make Meghann's blue turn even more purply.

So Meghann and I got a story ready. When we went down to breakfast—and Amy and Marcie had long since gotten up and gone down—Meghann was going to say she got it rolling off the sled down at the bottom. But everyone would think we meant it happened when we were all sledding together.

I wondered if Amy and Marcie would believe us though, if they would wonder why Meghann hadn't said something about it right then.

I hate keeping secrets from Amy. Usually we tell each other everything.

Well, anyway, I sure wasn't going to tell her this!

When we got downstairs, Mom and Dad made more of a fuss about Meghann's eye than Aunt Alice and Uncle Vinnie did, maybe because Mom and Dad felt responsible for Meghann as our guest.

Mom kept staring at Meghann. "Are you sure you're all right?" she said. "Does that hurt a lot?" And then she actually got up and came around the table to brush Meghann's bangs away to see better.

"No, it doesn't hurt, and I'm fine!" Meghann said, pulling away and smoothing down her bangs.

She wasn't. At least she didn't *look* fine. But I knew she didn't want to make a fuss over this. The less everybody talked about it, the better.

Then Dad chimed in, using his college-teacher voice. "Black eyes can be a sign of serious eye damage," he said, looking at Aunt Alice.

"I didn't bump my eye!" Meghann said. "I bumped my head."

"And there's quite a cut there," Mom said.

"I think she's all right," Aunt Alice said.

Uncle Vinnie looked across the table at Meghann. "She looks pretty good to me," he said. "A little like a prizefighter, actually."

Meghann made a face at him. "Funny!" she said.

Aunt Alice patted Meghann's hand. "Black eyes, broken bones—it's all a part of growing up," she said. "And I guess you've had your share this year."

That's one thing I like a lot about Aunt Alice and Uncle Vinnie—they don't get real upset about stuff. I wonder sometimes if that's why Meghann is such fun—that she doesn't have parents who hang over her all the time, worrying about her.

Not that Mom and Dad fuss over us too much. But they do worry.

But after Mom and Dad finally stopped fussing, they had this big announcement: All of us—Amy and me and Meghann and Marcie and Mikie and Bitsy and all our parents—we were all going to go to New York to Rockefeller Center to go ice-skating this afternoon! Even though we live in Connecticut, New York is just an hour away by train. Of course, we could have just gone skating on any of the ponds nearby that were frozen—except for the church hill one—but since the cousins don't get to go to New York very often, Mom and Dad thought it would be a nice treat for them.

Meghann and Marcie got so excited just thinking about actually being in New York that they immediately ran upstairs to see what they were going to wear.

And about two seconds later Meghann came racing back down, wailing, "How can I go to New York looking like this? With a black eye?"

So Aunt Alice took her upstairs and said she'd help with makeup, and Mom went too, and then Dad and Uncle Vinnie went with Mikie and Bitsy to the basement to dig out skates, leaving me at the breakfast table alone with Amy.

As soon as everyone was gone, Amy said, very quietly, "How did Meghann get a black eye?"

I shrugged and took a bite of my Cap'n Crunch. "I guess the way she said," I muttered.

"Falling off the sled?"

I nodded.

"When?" she asked.

"Amy!" I said. "She told you."

"You both went out last night after everyone was asleep, didn't you?" she said, very quietly.

"We did not!" I said.

I looked up and glared at her, but I could feel my face getting hot.

"Well, I think it's mean that you didn't let me come," Amy said, and she stood up and huffed off toward the stairs.

I watched her go, feeling kind of bad. Amy is my twin. My friend. We always do everything together!

So why hadn't I invited her last night?

"Amy!" I called to her.

She was already partway up the stairs, but she stopped.

"What?" she said.

"Come here!" I said.

"Why?" she said, still without turning around.

Well, what am I supposed to do, shout it?

"Because!" I said.

Slowly, she turned around and came back to the table. She didn't sit down, just stood there, hands in her jeans pockets, staring at me.

"Sit down!" I said.

"I don't want to sit down," she said. But she did.

I just looked at her, and she looked back.

"Okay," I said, very quietly. "Okay. We did go out."

"Then why didn't you ask me to come?"

Why didn't I? Because . . .

Maybe because last year I wouldn't have done that, gone out on the ice with a sled. And maybe . . . I don't know . . . maybe I didn't think Amy was like me anymore. She *wasn't* like me anymore. She obeyed all the rules. She got good grades and never got in trouble. She didn't care if we still had to dress like babies and couldn't wear lipstick—even chapstick. She didn't care at all about boys—only lizards.

She was just like I was last year!

I sighed. And maybe that's why she was still happy.

But how could I say that?

So I said the only real thing I could think of. "I thought you'd get mad," I said.

"Mad? Why would I get mad?" she said. "Last summer we snuck out all the time when we were staying at Meghann and Marcie's. And remember how last spring we snuck out to catch frogs?"

I shrugged. "It wasn't just the sneaking-out part," I said.

She just kept looking at me. "What?" she said.

"You won't tell?" I said.

She rolled her eyes.

"Okay, okay!" I said. Because I really knew she wouldn't.

I looked toward the back hall where the basement steps were. "We took the sleds out on the ice," I whispered. "On the pond."

"Ohmigosh!" she whispered. "Is that how she got a black eye?"

"No. She got that by slamming into a tree on the other side. It was awfully dark. And we were going awfully fast."

"Jennifer," Amy said. "You are dumb. Really. You could have gotten killed."

"Well, we didn't!" I said, smiling. Trying to smile. And trying to sound much more casual than I felt.

"Lucky," she said.

"Not lucky!" I said. "Smart. That pond's been frozen for months."

But I could feel fear hammering again at my chest, just as it had last night, when I stood there looking down the hill to the pond.

"But it's treacherous!" Amy said. "Mom and Dad

say that all the time. It's much worse than it looks. It's tricky!"

I shrugged. "How do they know that?" I said. "Because someone almost drowned there a zillion years ago?"

"Maybe. Maybe not," Amy said. "But they know."

"You act like parents know everything!" I said. "Like *you* know everything!"

"I know *some* things!" she said. "Not like some people I know."

I made a face at her.

Then told myself: Very mature, Jennifer.

Amy looked away and began picking at muffin crumbs on the tablecloth, pressing her finger down on them, then licking the squashed crumbs off her finger.

Gross.

"Jennifer?" she said after a minute, but without looking up at me. "Remember the other day you asked me if I'd help you with a project?"

I nodded. Of course I remembered. "Yup," I said.

"What was it?" Amy asked.

"Nothing special," I said.

"Then why'd you ask?"

I sighed.

Amy wiped her hands on her jeans and stood up. "I'm going upstairs," she said.

"Wait a minute!" I said. I stood up too.

She was glaring at me, her hands on her hips. I stood there glaring back at her, my hands on my hips.

57

It was like looking at myself in a mirror, practically. The outside of me.

"Okay," I said. "I did have a project. I wanted to try something."

"What?" she said. "That? Going out on the pond?"

"No!" I said.

She waited.

"It sounds stupid," I said.

"So?" she said.

I took a deep breath. "Don't laugh?" I said.

"I'm not laughing!" she answered.

"Okay," I said. "See, I want to have just one day when I'm in charge of me! When everything goes right because I'll make it go right."

"Why?" she said.

"Why, what?"

"Why do you want that?"

To show I can do it. To show I'm ...

I just shrugged. "Why not?" I said.

"Well, why do you want me to help you?"

Again I shrugged.

Why did I want Amy's help? Did I really need it? Yes.

"Because," I said slowly, "it wouldn't be . . . wouldn't be that great, I guess. Without you."

And in spite of everything, that was the truth.

CHAPTER
7

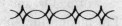

I read in a book once, *Space Station Seventh Grade,* that when kids grow up, they do it just opposite from other creatures in the natural world. For example, ugly little worms turn into beautiful butterflies. But kids growing up are like butterflies that turn into worms.

Boy, is that true! It was worm time for me. I felt exactly like a worm in Rockefeller Center that day.

Here are all these girls on the ice, these New York girls, and here's how they're dressed: First, they're wearing shiny, tight tights or else shiny, short skirts, black mostly (and Mom won't let me wear black till I'm sixteen, but some of these girls are even younger than me), short, swishy, shiny skirts that flip out around their bottoms when they twirl around, showing off most of their bottoms. The ones in skirts also wear flesh-colored tights that look like bare legs till you get up really close, unless you're lying on the ice looking up.

And how did I get to do that? More about that in a minute.

Then, to these skirts or tights, you add the top part, mostly more shiny, Lycra stuff, jackets that are so fitted you can see that the girls have something to show under them. (If I wore a top like that everyone would see that I'm still a worm. Or am I still a butterfly? Anyway, I guess I'm mixing metaphors or something here, but the point is I have no chest.)

Then there's this little headband—again, shiny. And shiny gloves.

Also, the ones in tights, guys, and girls too, some of their tights go all the way down and cover the tops of their skates, like stirrup pants for skates, so that it's all one long, shiny leg and skate.

Where do they buy all this shiny stuff? And I'm not allowed even one shiny sweater!

And that's the outfit, every one of them. Like something from the Olympic figure-skating that you see on TV.

But that's not the only similarity to the Olympic skaters. Because these girls—*they all know how to skate.*

Now, I know how to skate. You do it standing up straight, not bent over on your ankles. You push off, one foot in front of the other, and glide. Push, glide, push, glide. Sometimes you might even do circles. And me, when I'm feeling very confident, like at the end of winter, I can usually do a few push-glides, push-glides backward. But that's only at the end of the season and after lots of practice.

But the most important part of skating is that you have to learn how to duck the hockey pucks that the big kids shoot out on the ice all the time to scare off the rest of us so they can have the ice to themselves.

That's ice-skating in Connecticut.

In New York, this is how they do it:

Skate backward.

Leap!

Forward.

Twirl! Like a ballet dancer.

Circle around.

Link arms. Sometimes with another girl. Sometimes with a *boy*.

Skate backward, ponytails flying, little skirts flipping up in the wind or the breeze that they make just by skating.

Until they collide with a jerk like me who's decided to come out in the middle of the ice where the good skaters hang out and *skate backward*.

Which is why I know that those are not bare legs but flesh-colored tights.

And then this guy, this skating warden or something who works there specifically to help nerds like me who fall down—he comes whizzing out on the ice and pulls you up and you almost die of embarrassment.

But that wasn't even the most humiliating part. The most humiliating part was when Mom and Dad decided to skate together during the partners thing— that's when everybody has to get off the ice while just partners skate together to some soupy song that they pipe in over the loudspeaker. And then Amy got Marcie for *her* partner and *they* went out together. And Uncle Vinnie and Aunt Alice and even Bitsy and Mikie went out there!

I just know that all those people up on the steps and on that plaza overlooking the rink, they were just hysterical looking at our family.

Dad and Mom were both wearing ratty jeans that looked to be a hundred years old and bulky, long, down-filled coats that came practically to their ankles. Dad had brought along his old brown hockey skates, and Mom had white figure skates, but they were so old they weren't really white anymore but yellow. Aunt Alice had rented skates, but she was wearing ugly jeans too, the kind that old people wear with an elastic waist, jeans that were now white on the seat from her having fallen so many times. She was also wearing a borrowed jacket of Mom's that was too short in the arms for her. Uncle Vinnie didn't look too bad in his ski sweater and tight jeans, and he could have been okay except that he kept singing along to the music. Loudly. Mikie and Bitsy were giggling and falling down, and Mikie's hat had fallen over one ear and Bitsy kept trying to fix it for him, making it so that he could hardly see out anymore.

They looked like the Beverly Hillbillies!

I couldn't even watch.

I went inside to get a hot chocolate—a hot chocolate that I then found out cost *three* dollars!

Meghann's ankles were hurting, so she went in with me. ·

Inside, people were getting their skates off and doing stuff around their lockers. Cool-looking people. All of them.

Worm time.

"Meghann," I said, looking around that room. "Do you ever feel like a worm?"

She didn't say "Huh?" like Amy would have. She just said, "Why? Do you?"

I nodded. "Right now," I said. "Look how these people are dressed!"

She made a face. "Yeah."

"And look how we're dressed!" I said.

She looked down at herself. "I look okay," she said. She touched her forehead. "Except for my eye. Does it show much?"

"No," I said. "Not at all."

Liar! She looked more like a raccoon than a raccoon does. But it was a necessary lie. Or at least a kind one.

"Yeah," I said. "We're dressed okay for Connecticut. Or Virginia."

"What's the matter with Connecticut or Virginia?" she said.

I looked at her, squinting through the steam from my hot chocolate.

Did she really mean that question? Didn't she see the difference between the way our family was dressed and the way the rest of these people looked?

I just shrugged.

But then she said, "I know what you mean. But I thought it was just me who felt that way. You know, the way you feel when you go to a different school or something and everybody has different styles there—like when I started middle school this year and found out I was the only one still wearing tight jeans when they were all in those baggy ones, and I had to spend the whole first day of school hiding out in the girls' room. And then I got in trouble for missing classes."

"Exactly," I said. "And you feel like a worm."

She sighed and looked over at one of those fancy skaters who was standing by a locker, redoing her makeup. "Don't you wish you had one of those skating outfits?" she asked.

"Do you?" I said.

"Sure," she said. "Don't you?"

"Yes. And no."

"Why *no?*" she asked.

I sighed. "Because I'm not sure I'd look good in one."

"Everyone would look good in one."

I shook my head. "Bet," I said. "Me, I'd look like a . . . I don't know . . . like one of those toy poodles they dress up in the circus. You know, the ones they put tutus on? Skinny, spindly legs and a flat, poodle chest. That's me."

Meghann giggled. "Is not."

"Is too," I said.

Together, we stood there by the door, looking out at all those cool-looking people, all those beautiful people my age, when nobody I know is beautiful yet. Certainly not me. I heard Meghann sigh.

"Do you want to get out of here?" I asked.

"To go where?" she said.

"Shopping," I said. "There's got to be some neat shops around here. We could go to the stores and maybe buy earrings or something."

Although, come to think of it, I didn't have much earring money left after the hot chocolate.

"Yeah!" said Meghann. "I could get a New York souvenir." She frowned at me then. "We won't get kidnapped or something, will we?"

"Kidnapped?" I made a face at her.

She shrugged. "You know. You hear stuff about New York."

"People exaggerate," I said. But suddenly I realized that even though I wasn't really worried, probably Mom and Dad wouldn't like this much if they knew about it.

Well, they hadn't told me *not* to do it.

Both of us took off our skates, and Meghann, she returned hers and got the deposit back, and I tied mine together and hung them around my shoulder and we were ready to go.

I tried calling to Mom and Dad as they skated by, but it was so crowded on the ice and they were so far away that they didn't notice. Actually, I didn't wave and yell all that hard.

I looked up at the big clock.

You just get to go out on the ice for two hours, and there was still half an hour left.

I turned to Meghann. "We'll just go for half an hour," I said. "They won't care."

"Won't even notice," she said.

As we went up the stairs, she said, "I wonder what it feels like to live in New York."

"Crowded," I said.

We stood at the top of the steps, looking around the plaza at all the people, then up at the flagpoles where the different flags were being whipped around by the wind.

About a zillion people jostled by us, pushing and making their way in and out. Some of the people looked truly weird—I mean, I looked normal compared to them. There were three girls wearing long, lacy skirts and what looked like combat boots, and two guys with shaved heads, leather jackets, and earrings—but the earrings were in their *noses!* But the thing was, they all looked so confident! Maybe that was the secret? To look like whatever you wanted but to act as if you were the coolest person alive?

On one corner was a guy batting frantically at the air, as though there were a zillion mosquitoes buzzing around him. He wasn't wearing any coat or jacket, even though it was freezing out, but he did have on a fur hat and around his neck was something that looked like a dead dog—except I think it was one of those fur shawls like old ladies wear. He kept shadow-boxing with his mosquitoes or whatever they were and yelling loudly at them or at himself.

Right near him was another guy, talking very seriously *into his sleeve.* He wasn't weird looking like the boxer but kind of normal looking, in this regular grown-up suit and coat, except that ... oh, dopey me! He wasn't talking to his sleeve. He was talking on a portable phone. This little, tiny hand-held phone.

I poked Meghann. "Look at him. He must be important."

"Look at her," Meghann whispered back.

Right in front of us a lady was sitting on the side-walk, holding up a sign that said: "Homeless. Help get a hot meal." She had a little kitten curled up inside her coat, just its tiny head peeking out.

Was the kitten homeless too?

I looked at Meghann, and she looked at me.

If I gave the homeless lady anything I wouldn't have enough for my earrings.

But I could give her a little—maybe enough for a can of cat food?

Suddenly Meghann pointed.

She was looking across the street at a fancy shop, so fancy it had a doorman outside, just to open the door for people going in and out.

"Let's go!" Meghann said. "Let's see what's across the street."

I fished out a quarter and dropped it in the lady's box, and Meghann and I started across the street.

When we got near the store, though, we suddenly stopped short. The doorman was so snooty-looking, he was almost scary. He stood there absolutely still, staring straight ahead, not even blinking. His nose curved up at the end, and his chin was tilted up too. Nothing about him moved, except for his scarf, blowing a little in the wind.

"Is he real?" Meghann whispered.

I shrugged. I was almost certain I had seen him move before. But I also noticed that behind him, in the store window, were two mannequins that looked an awful lot like him.

As if he had heard Meghann's question, though, he suddenly put one hand up to adjust his scarf.

Meghann and I both stepped back, laughing.

"I don't think we can afford this place anyway," I said quietly. "Let's go look up the block."

She nodded, and we both started up the street, Meghann looking back over her shoulder.

"He was kind of cute," she said.

"Cute?" I said. "He looked like the Nutcracker. But hey! Look here!"

We stopped outside a jewelry shop with this fantastic display in the window, just one glittering jewel lying on a piece of black velvet, a spotlight shining on it.

"No way we can afford these places!" Meghann said. "Don't they have any shops like The Icing or anything?"

I shrugged. "Maybe," I said. "We have to keep on looking."

We went a few more blocks and turned two corners.

Each time we turned, I looked all around me and up at the street signs. No way was I getting lost in New York.

And then—oh, boy!—we saw it. My favorite kind of place. Meghann's favorite kind too. A bookstore! An enormous bookstore.

Both Meghann and I hurried in, glad to get out of the freezing cold. We headed for the back and the kids' books, especially the horror stuff that Meghann loved.

I looked at my watch. We'd already been gone ten minutes. That meant ten minutes back, so we could only spend ten minutes here.

After a few minutes, we each found a book we wanted, but I only had two dollars, so Meghann lent me the rest.

"Thanks," I said. "I'll pay you back. But we have to stick these in our pockets so our parents won't see. We can't tell them we left the rink."

"My pockets are huge," Meghann said. "Here!"

She took both books and put one in each pocket of her ski jacket.

Outside, we started back the way we had come, turning the first corner and going one block, then turning the next.

We walked for about ten minutes, at least ten minutes, the wind tearing at us, whipping up little pieces of paper and dirt and swirling them around our feet.

"Do you know where we are?" Meghann said after a while. "Shouldn't we be back there by now?"

"Nah," I said.

I looked at my watch.

Forty minutes! We'd been gone forty minutes.

"Yeah," I said.

I stopped and looked all around for a street sign but couldn't see any.

I looked up and down the street.

There were a zillion people and a zillion taxicabs and people selling things like hot dogs and hot chestnuts. But no flags for the rink. None at all. And no policemen either, no one to ask.

"We're lost, aren't we?" Meghann said.

I shrugged. "Not lost!" I said. "Just ..."

"Lost!" Meghann said. "I can tell."

I looked at my watch again. More than forty minutes. We were dead. If Mom and Dad found out we were running around New York, lost in New York, I'd be grounded for the rest of my life. Besides, I had to admit I was just a little bit scared. What if we were really lost?

A cab pulled up to the curb next to us and this lady got out, all wrapped up in furs, holding a tiny dog nestled against her, a red ribbon in her hair—the dog's hair.

"Meghann!" I said, suddenly getting an idea. "How much money do you have?"

She shrugged. "Some. I don't know."

"Five dollars?" I said. "Three dollars?"

"Probably," she said.

"Taxi!" I shouted. "Taxicab!"

I ran to the curb and pulled open the door of the cab that was still standing there.

A taxi couldn't cost more than five dollars, could it? We couldn't have come that far.

"Get in!" I said to Meghann.

She just stared at me.

"Get in!" I said again. To the driver, I said, "Can you take us to Rockefeller Center? Please?"

He looked over his shoulder at Meghann, who was climbing in, then at me, with my skates slung over my shoulder. "Skating rink, you mean?" he said.

"Yes," I said.

He didn't even answer, just pulled the flag down on the meter, the thing that told how much money the ride cost, and pulled away from the curb so fast that both Meghann and I were knocked back against the seat.

We lurched forward a block and then two, three blocks, and then stopped for a red light. Already the meter read two dollars and seventy cents.

Meghann looked at the meter, then at me.

"I'll pay you back," I said. "Don't worry."

"Pay me back?" Meghann whispered. "I don't know if I have enough."

"You don't have enough money?" I said.

"I don't know," she said. She dug out her wallet and opened it. I saw a couple of bills—all singles?

I looked again at the meter. It was clicking away, one number sliding out of sight, a higher one coming up. Just sitting at the red light, it had gone to two dollars and ninety cents.

Meghann took the bills out. Three ones. Three single dollar bills.

"That's it?" I said.

She nodded. "Can you go to jail if you don't pay?" she whispered.

I shrugged.

I dug into my pockets. I found fifty-three—no, fifty-four cents.

We went another block, and as we lurched around a corner, I looked again at the meter: three dollars and fifty cents.

"Is it far?" I said to the driver.

He slammed on the brakes for a red light and didn't answer, just pointed.

Up ahead, we could see the flags of Rockefeller Center, just about a block away.

"We'll get out here!" I said.

"Light's changed," he said, but before he could start up I had opened the door.

"Hey!" he yelled.

But we were already out and standing on the sidewalk.

Through the open cab door, Meghann thrust the three dollars in at him and I gave him the fifty-four cents.

I scrunched up my eyes and turned away fast.

A four-cent tip?

But we were out of there. Meghann slammed the cab door and we were racing up the block to the skating rink. Praying like mad that our parents hadn't yet noticed that we were gone.

CHAPTER
8

They hadn't noticed. Everyone had just come off the ice and were turning in their skates and all, so we hadn't even been missed. Still, for the rest of that afternoon, I was very quiet, and Meghann was too. I don't know what she was thinking, but I was afraid that if I said anything, it would come out—what had happened. So it wasn't until we were back home, and the four of us—Meghann and Marcie and Amy and me—were all piled on my bed that Meghann and I told them about it.

Only problem was, when Meghann told the story, she exaggerated a whole lot, saying things like the cab driver had gotten out of his cab and chased us, yelling and stuff. And she even said that the doorman held the door for us and smiled and asked where we were from.

That made Marcie really jealous. She kept shaking her head. "Lucky ducks!" she said. "You went shopping in New York alone and took a cab ride. And I bet anything you were flirting with the doorman."

She made a face at us, a very pouting kind of face.

Amy was mad and sulky too. She didn't say anything, not a single word, just kept giving me dirty looks.

I was pretty sure I knew what she was thinking: Not only had Meghann and I had this fun thing in New York—well, sort of fun, exciting, anyway—but we'd snuck out to go sledding last night.

Leaving her out.

Two times.

Well, we couldn't help what happened today, could we? I mean, we hadn't planned that to happen.

I flopped down on my back, letting my head hang off the edge of the bed, my hair trailing on the floor. Doing that always reminds me of when Amy and I were little, how we'd pretend the house was upside down, and we could walk on the ceiling.

I didn't want Amy mad at me. And I would never tell her that it had been more fun with Meghann than with her—at least today and last night.

But that reminded me of what I had said that morning—how I needed Amy.

Should I tell the others about my plan now, about having a day when we could all be totally in charge? Maybe even Meghann could persuade her mom to persuade my mom to go away for a few days, and that way we could *really* have a day with no one to boss us around.

I sat up, closing my eyes for a minute to let the dizzy feeling go away.

Hanging head down might be all right for Amy's lizards, but it sure made me feel weird.

When I opened my eyes, Amy was still sulking and Marcie was too.

Meghann just looked at me and shrugged, like: What's the matter with them?

Although she must have known.

"I have an idea," I said. "I have a plan for this week. Want to hear?"

"To do more stuff without us?" Marcie said.

"No, not to do stuff without you!" I said. "Just the opposite. Although I won't tell you if you're both going to sulk!"

"Who's sulking?" Marcie said.

"I am!" Amy said.

I had to smile at that.

For just a minute, it seemed that Amy started to smile back at me, but then she put her mad face back on again.

"What's your plan?" Marcie said.

"Well," I said, "it's something Amy and I have been talking about doing."

I looked at Amy.

No response.

"Except Amy's being a pain," I added.

Still nothing.

"Amy!" I said.

"What?" she said back.

"Stop being a pain!" I said.

"A pain?" she said. "Look who's . . ."

But she didn't finish whatever it was she was about to say. Because at that moment our door burst open, and Bitsy and Mikie both came charging in.

Bitsy was carrying her Barbie doll, and Mikie had Bitsy's Ken doll, and they were both yelling something. Yelling is usual for Bitsy, but Mikie is usually so quiet you hardly know he's around—but not now.

They were both arguing about something, each of them trying to tell us whatever it was before the other one got a chance.

Bitsy was jumping up and down, all breathless, her curls bouncing around her face. "Me!" she shouted. "I said I'd tell!"

As she stood there glaring at Mikie, he very calmly turned to Amy and me and said, very fast and very quiet, *"Your* mom and dad are going away for the weekend and *our* mom and dad are going to stay here with us."

And that's when Bitsy hit him with her Barbie doll.

Then, very calmly, Mikie turned back and bopped Bitsy over the head with the Ken doll.

Then both of them started howling.

"Bitsy!" I said. "Come here! And don't hit!"

"Come here, Mikie!" Amy said, holding out her arms. "It's all right."

But Mikie went flying out the door, yelling for his mom. And Bitsy went running, sobbing, "Mommy!"—probably afraid that he'd tell his version of the story first.

Downstairs we could hear them howling and both sets of parents trying to soothe them.

I thought: Maybe Amy and I aren't much different from the little kids.

I got up and shut the door, then came back and sat on the bed. "Okay," I said, deciding not to wait for Amy to make up with me, the first time that had happened in a long time. "My idea was to try and have one day when we could get to do anything we wanted, without adults bossing us around. Wouldn't that be cool? Just to plan one day like that?"

"Adults are always around to boss you," Meghann said.

"Not if Mom and Dad go away," I said.

"My mom and dad aren't going away," Meghann said.

"Still," I said. "Your parents don't have to know everything we're doing. I don't mean we should plan anything really bad. I just meant we decide on what we'd like to do if there were nobody around. And try to do it. Or get it. For just one day. There's a zillion things I'd do if it weren't for parents."

"Me too," Marcie said, seeming to forget that just

a minute ago she'd been mad at me. "I'd stay up all night and watch R-rated videos. I've been dying to see *Nightmare on Elm Street,* but Mom has fits when I even mention it."

"I'd get my ears pierced," Meghann said. "And then I'd go shopping and buy one of those skating outfits."

"Where would you use it in Virginia?" Marcie asked.

Meghann shrugged. "Who cares? I just want one."

"Cool," Marcie said. "Get anything we want for one whole day. But you know what? That would never happen. Parents never let you do anything you want."

"Our parents are going away," I said, looking over at Amy, who was still sulking. "Amy? What would you do if you could do anything you want?"

"Get a new lizard," she muttered.

Really? Well, at least she'd answered.

"So want to plan it?" I said. "If it's true Mom and Dad are going away for a weekend? We could do all sorts of stuff that we couldn't do if they were here."

"But what about my parents?" Meghann said. "Mom would never let me get my ears pierced."

"Compromise!" I said, grinning at her. "Maybe not your ears pierced, but I bet you could get something you wanted. We'll get the videos Marcie wants. We'll eat pizza for breakfast. We'll all decide together."

"I know!" Meghann said suddenly. "I'm president of the Cousins' Club! I get to decide what we do for one whole day."

"No way!" I said. "It was my idea."

Meghann just smiled. "Sorry. I'm president."

"And I thought of it," I said.

"So?" She just looked at me.

"Unh-uh!" I said. "I thought of it. We all decide together."

We glared at each other.

"Jen's right," Amy said after a minute. "It was her idea."

Meghann turned to Amy. "No fair!" she said. "You two always side with each other."

Ha! Where had she been for the last hour?

"I'm not taking sides," Amy said. "I just think nobody should boss anybody. We decide together what we want to do for one whole entire day. It's only fair."

"That's what I think too," Marcie said.

Meghann made a big, huffy breath. But after a minute, she shrugged. "But I am president!"

"We know!" I said. "But we're all going to do this together. Okay?"

"Okay," Meghann said, with a big sigh.

"Then let's plan it," I said.

And we did. Planned one absolutely terrific day.

CHAPTER
9

Next morning, all four of us—Meghann, Marcie, Amy, and me—were in the video store looking around, deciding which videos we'd choose for our special day. But the excuse—that is, the excuse we gave our parents for going to the video store that particular day—was to get a video for Bitsy and Mikie. Dad had driven us there and was waiting for us outside in the car, reading the morning paper, *The New York Times*—without which, Dad says, he cannot live.

I secretly think Dad was happy to have a minute to himself, with the little kids home with Mom and Aunt Alice and Uncle Vinnie, and us in the video store. He kept saying before we went in, "Just take your time. No hurry at all."

So we did—take our time, that is. We each went to

different areas of the store: Meghann to the R stuff, Marcie to the other R stuff, the horror stuff, and Amy to the regular stuff she loves, like *The Secret Garden* and *Anne of Green Gables.* Me, I took a minute to really look for something for Bitsy because one of us had to do it.

We had stayed up half the night talking about our plans. We had agreed on some things, and the date we had picked was Friday and maybe Saturday too—the next-to-last days of our vacation, the days Mom and Dad would be away. Mom and Dad would leave early Friday morning for an overnight stay at an inn in the mountains and would be coming back Saturday night. They wouldn't be back till very, very late though, so we'd have two whole days and almost two nights.

On our list we had some cool stuff, like skating, sledding—but not out on the pond—eating anything we wanted, like pizza and no broccoli, staying up all night, watching R-rated videos (there was a horror one I've wanted for ages and I was going to look for it in a minute), talking on the phone with no time limit, wearing lipstick.

But there was another too, a more secret thing. We had each decided to keep one thing to ourselves, one thing we wanted that we wouldn't tell each other till the night before. It didn't have to be something we thought we could actually get—just some wish, even an impossible one. Like Meghann's getting her ears pierced.

It was Meghann's idea to keep that one thing secret—and it made me wonder what hers was. I bet anything it wasn't pierced ears. Was it anything like mine?

There were problems too—like how to get R-rated videos and not have Aunt Alice and Uncle Vinnie know what we got. And we also kept fighting over who would get to choose the food—pizza or MacDonald's. We hadn't told the grown-ups about our plan, but we had said that on Saturday there were some special things we wanted, and they had agreed to give us the card for the video store and to buy whatever we wanted for dinner and snacks. I don't think the dinner part was particularly because they wanted to make us happy, but because with Mom and Dad gone, that meant nobody had to cook.

But the best thing of all was that Amy and I weren't mad at each other anymore. I think Amy was happy just to see me happy and including her in everything, just like always. (I was beginning to think that she gets upset if I'm grumpy because she thinks something's wrong with me, just like secretly I think there's something wrong with her because she's always so calm and cool.)

Anyway, it was cool planning our day, although the secret thing was worrying me a little, the thing that I didn't want to tell anyone about yet: Robert Stagnaro. Could I include him? Or would he wreck the whole day?

And if he wouldn't wreck it, how could I arrange it? And what would the others say when I told them? I mean, I knew I could tell Meghann. But Amy?

Maybe I could just casually suggest that he come sledding with us? That wouldn't be like a date or anything.

Or I could invite him over to watch a video.

Right. An R-rated video?

Well, we could just get a regular one.

But how? Pick up the phone and call him?

No way.

I was going back and forth like this, having this argument or discussion with myself, when I suddenly found the video I'd been looking for for Bitsy: *Beauty and the Beast.*

I held it up, looking around for Amy, and that's when I saw him—not the Beast, but Robert.

He was standing on the other side of the display from me with his best friend, Judd, who *is* a beast. He's one of those weird boys who makes noises. I think he doesn't even know he's doing it half the time. Like some people give off a certain smell—well, Judd gives off sounds. He's either cracking his knuckles or making big belching sounds, or else he's making cheek noises—puffing out his pudgy cheeks and then smacking them so hard that the air blows out and sounds like a fart. That's what he was doing then and that's how come I looked up and noticed him. And noticed Robert.

Right away I dropped *Beauty and the Beast,* because I didn't want him to think I was getting that for myself! And then I turned and tried to hide.

I don't know exactly why I did that, except that I hate to meet people in places other than the place they're supposed to be. I mean, if this was school, okay. But here? Not.

Weird, I know.

Anyway, I turned away and grabbed the first thing I could get my hand on, just to pretend to be interested in something and to keep my head bent, when I heard Amy.

"Hey, Jennifer!" she yelled.

You could hear her in Virginia, the way she yelled.

I scrunched down further. I took the video I had picked up, stuck it under my chin, and knelt down, pretending to be tying my sneaker lace.

"Jennifer!" she yelled again. "Come here. Look what I found. *Bambi!"*

Oh, great.

I stayed hidden.

Oh, please, please let her shut up or disappear or something.

But no—I heard her calling again.

And then she goes, "Oh, hi Robert. Have you seen Jennifer?"

And he goes, "Yeah, she was over there with *Beauty and the Beast,* but she disappeared."

I almost fell over. I did fall over—well, back onto my seat. He had *seen* me? He had *noticed* me?

Oh, man! And noticed me with *Beauty and the Beast.* And Amy was yelling about *Bambi.*

Was it better to stand up right then and tell him that we were looking for videos for our baby sister? Or should I just pretend to be dead?

And did my hair look as bad as I thought it looked? I hadn't even bothered to blow it dry this morning, had just put it up in a ponytail while it was still wet from the shower.

I dropped the video in my lap, then reached up and frantically undid the ponytail, using my fingers for a comb. Then I redid the whole thing. And almost got stepped on by Meghann, who came around the corner of the display case with Marcie.

"What are you doing down there?" Marcie said.

"Shush up!" I whispered.

"Are you all right?" Meghann said.

I nodded, then pointed toward the display case. "Robert!" I mouthed.

"Who?" Marcie said.

"Oh!" Meghann said, her eyes wide. She poked Marcie. "Shush!" she said. "It's Robert."

"Who's Robert?" Marcie said, and then both of them stood on tiptoe to look over the display case at him.

I tugged at Meghann's jeans. "Don't look!" I said.

"Why?" she said, crouching down beside me. "Is it the fat one?"

"No!" I said.

"Oh, good," she said.

"I don't want him to see me," I said.

"How come?"

"You know!"

"Oh," she said again.

And then, like this whole thing wasn't stupid enough, Amy arrived, came around the corner carrying two videos—*Bambi* and *The Little Mermaid*—one in each hand, waving them like wands.

"Oh, there you are!" she said. I found *Bambi* and *The Little Mermaid,* but I think . . . What are you sitting on the floor for?"

"Hiding, I think," Marcie said.

"Hiding!" Amy said.

"Will you hush up?" I hissed at her. And then very loud I said, "I'm looking for . . . I dropped my . . . contact lens!"

I didn't drop my contact lens. I don't wear contact lenses. I don't even wear glasses! Why had I said that? It had just popped into my head.

I heard a loud laugh from the other side of the display then—two laughs. And some hooting and shuffling. "Contact lens!" Judd yelled. "Get it? *Contact?"* And then he made another sound, a smacking sound, like an exaggerated kiss.

I could feel tears spring to my eyes.

Amy and Marcie and Meghann just stood there staring down at me.

"Contact lens?" Amy said, and she reached out a hand to pull me up, but I shook my head.

I bent my head then so nobody would see—but with my head bent, the tears spilled over and one splashed right down in my lap.

On my lap while I sat here on the floor like a jerk! Hiding. And he knew it.

And Judd thought I wanted to kiss him!

Then I heard more noises, coming closer—the squelching, squishing noises that could only be Judd, and then those kissy, smacky noises. I wasn't looking up but I could see his feet. He came around the display case, and Robert's feet were right behind him, and if they had come any closer, they would have stepped on us.

"Whoa!" Judd said, and I looked up and saw him backing up, pretending to be falling backward, waving his arms in circles like he was trying to catch his balance.

He stepped on Robert's foot and Robert shoved him and they both fell backward and they were both laughing and Judd made a particularly loud smacky-lip noise.

Die. It was the only thing to do. Die.

Or disappear.

But how?

Run. I dropped the video. I stood up. I kept my head bent and then I ran. Ran around the display case, around the opposite way from where they were all standing. Ran out the door of the video store and around the corner to where Dad had parked.

I opened the car door, jumped in the front seat, and slammed the door and then locked it.

Dad looked up from his newspaper. "Uh-oh," he said.

Then, without another word, he held out his arms to me—both arms.

I don't remember moving toward him, but suddenly I was in his arms. He held me close to him, the newspaper crushed between us, him not asking me anything, not saying anything.

He just held me and I put my head against his rough, tweedy jacket, and it prickled and hurt my cheeks, but it felt good too, and I cried. And cried. And cried.

Dad hugged me and rocked me, just the way he used to do when I was really, really little.

I just cried my eyes out.

He rocked and rocked and rocked me. He kept going, "Hush now, hush," even though I wasn't saying anything, and then he whispered, "I know, I know."

What did he know? I sure didn't know.

Except I knew one thing: I had been a jerk.

Oh, why hadn't I just stayed where I was when I saw Robert? Why hadn't I just said "Oh, hi Robert," just as cool as Amy had, and then I could have gone over to see what Amy was looking at and we could have decided between *Beauty and the Beast* and *Bambi* or else *The Little Mermaid* and maybe I could have even gone back and asked Robert if he ever went sledding on the church hill . . .

But I didn't. And now I couldn't. Because I was an absolute jerk!

For a long time, Dad just held me, me crying into his chest and getting his jacket all wet, him patting my back. Eventually, though, I stopped crying. And still, Dad kept patting me and he didn't ask one single thing.

All he did was say, "I know, I know," like maybe he really did know. And after a while, he handed me his handkerchief.

Then, when the others eventually came out of the video store and got in the car, very quiet and subdued, Dad just told them that I wasn't feeling very well.

And that was sure the truth.

CHAPTER 10

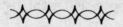

So what did that all prove? That's what worried me. It was like you could start off with a perfectly okay day like today—and then get it messed up with something that you had no control over.

Or did you?

I sighed. I could have done something different, I knew. I could have done all those things that I'd told myself about, sitting there in the car with Dad.

But I *couldn't* have done those things or I'd have done them. And that's what made me feel like crying again.

Now how was I going to face Robert in school?

Maybe we could move. Dad could take a job at another college. The University of Alaska was always looking for people—I remember hearing Dad tell

Mom that once. And Mom's work as an illustrator can be done anywhere.

There are only Eskimos in Alaska probably. And at least with them, when they kiss, they don't make any smacky sounds.

Maybe we wouldn't have to move, though. Amy said Robert hadn't even seemed to notice anything, that he and Judd got into a shoving match and the manager came over and threatened to throw them out, so they just stopped and went back to picking out videos.

I didn't believe that for a minute. I mean, I believed the manager threatened to throw him out. But I didn't believe that he hadn't noticed the dumb things I did.

There was one good thing that happened after that, though: I didn't have even one more minute of wishing for a boy. I crossed that off my list and, even better, I could feel relieved because I had no big secret that I was worried about when it was time to share our lists.

Boys were gross.

I did wonder about Dad, though. I mean, he was really pretty cool. Could he ever have been like Robert and Judd?

I didn't think he could have been. And I couldn't find out from Mom because she hadn't met Dad until they were both in graduate school, when they were already old, so she couldn't know if he was as weird as the boys I knew.

This whole thing did make my attempt at a perfect day seem a little silly though, since along comes a boy and everything is ruined.

Except then I went back to my first thought: No boys.

And that was my plan: N. O. Boys. For a long time.

It wasn't hard to do, either. For the next two days, I didn't think about a boy once, except to be mad at Arthur Lamb and Peter Bravo, who were hogging all the good spots on the sledding hill.

On the night before Mom and Dad were leaving, the night before our planned day, all of us—Mom and Dad and Aunt Alice and Uncle Vinnie and the little kids and Amy and Meghann and Marcie and me—all of us settled down in the living room to play some games and watch a video. Dad had gone back to the video store and got *Beauty and the Beast* for the little kids. We had all seen it about a zillion times, but Bitsy can never see it too much. We should have bought it— could have bought it—for all the times we'd rented it.

Anyway, that night Mikie and Bitsy were sprawled side by side on the rug, watching *Beauty and the Beast* and playing with Legos. Seeing them playing like that together and talking about the video and singing some of the songs together—and wrestling with each other and then occasionally hugging each other—I couldn't help thinking that little boys are so totally different from big ones.

Little girls too, I guess.

Marcie and Amy and Aunt Alice decided to play Boggle, and Mom and Dad and Uncle Vinnie and me settled down to play Pictionary.

I love Pictionary. This is how the game works:

You do it in two teams. One person on a team picks a card and the card has a word on it—for example, the word *beautiful.*

That person shows the card to one person on the *other* team—but not on their own team. Then each of the people who have looked at the card, their job is to draw a picture for their own partner, a picture that will suggest the word *beautiful.* You can't use motions or gestures or spellings—just pictures. So how do you draw a picture that shows *beautiful?*

Not easy!

There's also a time limit and a timer. The team who guesses first, before the timer runs out in like two minutes, is the winner.

Of course, playing this game against Mom, who is an artist, might seem like she had an unfair advantage—except that Mom gets so carried away with her drawing that by the time she's finished, the other team has usually guessed and won.

This time Dad chose me as a partner, and Mom and Uncle Vinnie were partners on the other team.

Uncle Vinnie held out the box to me. "You first, Jen," he said. "Pick a card."

I picked a card, studied it a minute, then handed it to Uncle Vinnie.

Worried, was the word. I sure knew how it felt to be worried. But how was I going to draw it?

Uncle Vinnie frowned at the card, nodded, then picked up the timer.

"Ready?" he said, looking at me.

I nodded, and he turned over the timer, and we each picked up our pencils.

My first thought was to draw a boy—they make you worry, don't they? But how would Dad guess that? Then I had another thought. Twins. I quickly drew two little stick figures, side by side. Twins.

A twin makes you worry. My twin sure made me worry.

Dad caught on right away. Sort of. But instead of "Worry," he said, "Twins!"

I nodded and made gestures to show him he was on the right track—you're allowed to do that. But then he said, "Amy! Girl! Two girls!"

I shook my head and tried to think.

What would show *worry?*

Next to me, I could hear Mom laughing.

"A . . . a . . . an accident?" she was saying. "Airplane! I know, airplane accident. Airplane falling out of the sky. Sky? No, clouds? No!"

Uncle Vinnie was poking the paper so hard with his pencil that he was making holes in it.

Well, I guess an airplane falling out of the sky would make you worry, wouldn't it?

But how could I . . .

I knew! *Worry*—frown! I drew a big frown on the face of one of my twins.

"Cut?" Dad said. "An accident? Blood?"

I shook my head hard, sat back, and looked at my drawing. Cut? How could this look like a cut? It was a frown!

"Meghann's black eye!" Dad said.

Right. Like that would be in the game cards.

Carefully, I drew a downturned line on the other twin, a careful, downturned line all the way across her head.

"Headache?" Dad said.

Good thing I wasn't thinking of being an artist when I grew up.

"Time's up!" Uncle Vinnie said.

I dropped my pencil.

"Worry!" I said to Dad. "Couldn't you see? Look—worry, frown?"

"Oh," Dad said. "But there's two of them."

I shrugged. "Well, sure. They're twins. You know, worry."

"Oh!" Dad said again. But it wasn't "Oh!" like in "Oh, I see!" Just "Oh."

I turned to Uncle Vinnie. "Why were you showing an airplane accident?"

He laughed and looked sheepish. "Airplanes are the only thing I know how to draw," he said.

"Fighter planes!" Dad said. "You drew fighter planes all the time when you were a little kid." He reached over and punched Uncle Vinnie lightly on the arm.

Mom laughed. "A terrible artist," she said.

Dad laughed too. "But a pretty good brother," he said.

I looked at Dad and Uncle Vinnie then, each smiling at the other, and tried to picture them as brothers, as little kids together.

What were they like then? Did they fight the way Amy and I do? Did they sneak out at night and do stuff they weren't supposed to do? Did they tell each other secrets?

Did one grow up faster than the other one, and did that make one of them mad? Or sad?

It was so hard to picture parents as kids.

We played some more rounds then, Dad doing the drawing at times, then me.

Dad is even worse at drawing than I am. But I'm good at guessing, so we win more when he draws—I guess because I know how his mind works better than he knows how mine works.

After about an hour, it was clear that Dad and I were the winners.

"Another round?" Uncle Vinnie said. "Switch partners?" He smiled at me. "You and I can beat them easy!" he said.

"Not if all you can draw is airplanes," I said.

But nobody wanted to play anymore, not even Mom and Dad. Everybody, Amy and Marcie and Meghann and Aunt Alice, everybody had sort of set aside their games and were watching *Beauty and the Beast.* Even I was half watching it, although I had seen it a zillion times already. I know it's a little kid's video, but I just love Beast—love him, but hate the part that was coming, the part where he turns into the Prince. It's not just because I hate princes, either, because they're boys. It's because Beast is much nicer as a beast. He's sort of gruff and mean and grumpy, but you know, because you can actually see, from the way he acts, that he's really lovable.

When he turns into the Prince, he acts like a jerk.

I got up and stretched. I couldn't stand the dumb way he was looking at Belle.

Or the dumb way Belle was looking back at him with the same dumb look.

I went out in the kitchen and switched on the light, then opened the refrigerator door and stood there looking in. What did I want? A coke? Juice? Chocolate milk?

Nah.

I closed the door and went to the cabinet.

Cookies?

No.

Chips?

Amy came in and stood beside me. She reached past me and took out the package of chips.

"I can't stand the Prince," she said, opening the chips and taking a handful and dropping them one by one into her mouth, her head tipped back. "He's such a nerd."

"Really," I said.

I took the chips away from her, took a handful, then jumped up on the counter to eat them.

"Why do you think so?" she asked.

I shrugged. "Same reason as you, I guess."

"He's much nicer as Beast," she said.

"I know," I said. "Much."

She went over and jumped up on the counter opposite me. She held out her hands, and I tossed her the bag of potato chips.

"You think we'll ever act like that?" she said.

"Like what?" I asked. "Belle and the Prince?"

"Yeah," she said.

"Nah," I said. "Never. You?"

She screwed up her face.

Then she sighed, and when she spoke she sounded perfectly disgusted but, as usual with Amy, perfectly honest.

"Yeah," she said. "Probably."

CHAPTER
11

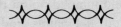

Before we went up to bed that night, we said goodbye to Mom and Dad because they were going to be gone by five in the morning. They were catching a six A.M. commuter flight to Burlington, Vermont, to go cross-country skiing and to stay at an inn up there in the woods. They would ski all day Friday and Saturday, then come back on a late flight Saturday.

Leaving us to have two days—and tomorrow was the special one we'd planned.

When we said goodnight, both Mom and Dad had about a thousand instructions. They also papered the refrigerator with notes: doctors' numbers, pharmacy numbers, the number of the inn they'd be at, their flight information.

You'd think they were leaving for a year.

And they gave us about a thousand kisses, and Mom even looked teary.

"It's only for one night, Mom!" I said.

"I know," Mom said. "But it's hard to leave you kids. You'll understand when you're a mother yourself."

Ha! Like I'd ever be that. Because first you had to get married.

When Dad said goodbye, he held me away from him for a minute and looked at me. "Things better now?" he asked, very softly.

The first reference he had made to that day in the car.

I nodded.

He pulled me close and gave me an extra squeeze.

And then we all said goodnight, and the four of us, Amy and Meghann and Marcie and me, raced upstairs.

Now was the time we had planned to share our secrets—the one secret thing we wanted if we could have a perfectly wonderful day—the very next day.

In my room, we sat on my bed, each of us with our list. I think we were all a little nervous—all but me. No bad secrets for me.

Meghann had to go first, because she was president of the Cousins' Club. It was probably a little mean, but that's what the three of us had voted. Three to one.

"Go, Meghann!" Marcie said now.

"Okay," she said. "But you have to promise something first."

101

She had folded her list over and over, so now it was no more than a little crumpled ball in her hand.

"What?" Amy said.

"That you won't laugh," Meghann said.

"Of course we won't!" Amy said.

"I will," Marcie said.

But you could tell she was just joking.

"Jennifer?" Meghann said.

"I won't," I said.

"Okay," Meghann said. She took a deep breath. "If I could be—I mean, get—anything I wanted for a day, you know what? I'd . . ."

She crumpled up the paper. "Nope!" she said. "You'll laugh!"

"Won't!" I said. "We just promised."

"Unh-uh!" Meghann said.

Amy rolled her eyes. "I'll go," she said. "If you don't laugh at me, you won't laugh at anybody."

I know we were all relieved at that. It's always best to have someone else tell their deepest secrets first and to see the reactions.

"Okay," Amy said. "A great day for me would be all the stuff we talked about, videos and pizza and all that. And . . ."

She looked across the room toward her lizard cages.

A long pause.

"And what?!" Meghann said.

"Tell us," Marcie said.

"Come on!" I said.

Everybody laughed.

"A lizard!" Amy said. "I'd get this incredible lizard."

"Huh?" I said.

"A lizard?" Marcie said. "You've got about a thousand lizards. Why's that a secret?"

"A lizard that sings!" Amy said. "One that could . . . you know . . . communicate? Just like dolphins? That's what I really, really want."

"You do?" Meghann said.

Amy nodded.

"Oh," Meghann said.

"You're kidding," Marcie said. "Lizards don't sing. And what would you want one for anyway even if it did?"

Amy just shrugged.

Marcie shook her head, and I could see she was about to laugh.

"Weird," she muttered.

I looked over at Amy. Her face got really red.

"That's not nice, Marcie," I said.

"But she wants a singing lizard!" Marcie said, as if I hadn't heard Amy myself. "A lizard that talks to her. Why would anybody want that? Even if there was such a thing as a talking lizard."

"I didn't say a *talking* lizard!" Amy said angrily. But she also sounded a little like she was near tears. "I said a lizard that could communicate. And you know what? Nobody said it had to be something that you could get. It was *wished*. That's all."

"Right," I said. And then, because Amy looked sad and Marcie was staring at her, I said, "My turn."

Marcie and Meghann turned to me.

I took a deep breath. "Okay," I said. "Actually, I crossed this off my list because I changed my mind because of ... of something that happened. But my secret was ..."

I snuck a look over at Amy.

She was blinking hard.

I took another breath and went on, very slowly, giving her time to get the tears totally blinked away. "Well, see," I said, "my secret was to have—I mean, to include, a boy. Not a boyfriend!" I added quickly. "Just a boy who I'd like to go sledding with. Or something."

Both Marcie and Meghann were watching me closely.

I could feel myself blushing.

"But I don't want that anymore!" I added.

"How come?" Meghann asked.

I shrugged.

"Because of what happened in the video store, I bet!" Marcie said, laughing. "Because he knew you were hiding and he knew you don't wear contact lenses."

I glared at her.

I had no idea she could be so ... what? Not nice? Insensitive or something?

"So what's *your* secret?" I said, mean-sounding.

Let her see how it felt to be laughed at.

"I'd get a horse," she said, very calmly. "A pony."

"A pony!" I said. And for some reason that made me extra mad, because I wanted to be able to ... to laugh at her or something.

But how could I laugh? I'd like a pony too. I've always wanted my own horse.

"Now you have to go," Marcie said to Meghann. "You're the last one left."

Meghann scrunched her list even further into a ball. I saw her glance quickly at Amy, then back at us. "Okay," she said. "If I had a perfect day, I'd ... I'd get an entire new wardrobe. I'd throw away every single thing I owned. And . . ."

"That's not a *real* secret," Marcie said.

Meghann just shrugged. "Is too!" she said. "I told one, and that's all I have to do."

"Chicken!" Marcie said. "You have another secret and you're a chicken. I bet it's even more weird than a singing lizard."

Meghann made a face at her.

Marcie slid off the bed. "I have to go to the bathroom," she said.

"Me too," Meghann said, sliding off the bed too.

"Me first!" Marcie said.

"I'm coming with you," Meghann said.

"I don't want you with me!" Marcie said. "Can't I have some privacy?"

But Meghann followed Marcie out into the hall anyway, and I heard them talking quietly—Meghann talking.

I hoped she was telling Marcie to stop being a big jerk.

"Amy?" I said when they were gone.

Amy didn't answer.

I got up and went across the room to the lizard cages.

I bent over and scooped up one of the lizards—the redheaded one, the only one that didn't dart away from me—and brought it to her.

She didn't smile or say thank you or anything.

But she did take it from me and began stroking it with one finger.

I sat down on the bed across from her.

"Amy, it's okay," I said. "I think a lizard that sings would be cool. If it could communicate with you or something."

"Yeah," Amy said with a sigh.

"Don't worry about it," I said. "Marcie can be a jerk sometimes."

"She thought I was weird," Amy said.

"Well, you're not," I said. But it came out kind of tentative-sounding. I mean, I'm always thinking that Amy is weird. Nice, but weird.

"You're not!" I said again, more firm-sounding this time. "You're not weird."

"Marcie thinks so," she said again.

"So?" I said.

Amy sighed, a big, trembly breath. "Sometimes I do too," she said.

"You do too, what?" I said.

"Think I'm weird," she said.

"You do?" I said.

She nodded.

"Know what?" I said.

"What?" she said.

"I do too."

She looked up at me, surprised-looking.

"I don't mean that I think *you're* weird," I said. "I mean that I sometimes think I'm weird."

"Unh-uh," Amy said, shaking her head hard. "Not you. You're normal."

Me, normal? Ha!

We both sat there looking at one another.

I don't know exactly what Amy was thinking—but I know what I was thinking: I may not be completely weird, but I'm surely not normal.

Is it normal to want boys to like you when you hate them? Is it normal to see a guy you like in the store and then hide from him and then cry your eyes out? Is it normal to get lousy grades when you used to get all *A*s when you were little—like Amy was still getting? Was it normal to feel like you'd never be completely happy again, at least until you were all grown up and nobody could boss you around? Was it normal to break all the rules that your parents trusted you for and to risk your own life and your cousin's life too? And then tell lies about it?

And the worst: Was it normal to be having all these things happening to you when they weren't happening to your twin—your *identical* twin?

What *was* normal?

I got up off the bed and started to get undressed.

When Marcie and Meghann came back in the room, we were all very quiet.

Amy put her lizard in its cage and we all got ready for bed and turned out the lights, none of us talking or anything.

For a long time I lay in the dark, wide awake, thinking.

Across the room, I pictured Amy and Marcie, awake too, lying side by side, mad at each other, each thinking her own mad thoughts.

Next to me, Meghann lay very still, but I could tell she wasn't sleeping either.

I bet anything she was thinking, just like I was, maybe thinking about that secret she hadn't shared with us.

And then, lying there thinking about Meghann thinking, I suddenly had this thought, this truly weird thought: What was it like to be Meghann? Or Marcie? Or even Amy? I mean, what's it *really* like to be someone else?

Weird to realize other people are walking around inside their own selves, thinking their own thoughts—and to realize you can never *really* feel what it's like to be them. But they know what it's like to be them. And they don't know what it's like to be you.

Really, really weird.

And that's the last thought I had before I fell asleep: weird. Maybe it's not just Amy and me who feel weird. Maybe the whole world is really, truly weird.

CHAPTER 12

Maybe it was good that we had that sort-of fight that night, because it made us all much nicer and friendlier and even kinder to one another next morning—the beginning of our special day.

Marcie was especially friendly to Amy, offering to bring her breakfast in bed! And even though Amy said no thanks, I could tell she knew Marcie was trying to make up.

Meghann and I traded sweaters when we got dressed, and Meghann showed me how to make my hair in a ponytail like hers, pulled way over to one side.

I studied myself in the mirror.

Not bad. I wondered what Robert would think.

When we went downstairs, Mom and Dad were already gone, and Aunt Alice and Uncle Vinnie had made us this huge breakfast of French toast and pancakes and eggs any way we wanted them and Pop Tarts and doughnuts.

Not cold pizza, but maybe better.

I ate so much I didn't think I'd eat another bite again, ever.

Except that by lunchtime we were all starved because we had been out sledding on the hill all morning—sledding that wasn't even a little bit ruined by the big boys because they were all across the street on the other pond playing ice hockey. And who cared if they broke each other's heads open with the hockey puck?

For lunch, Uncle Vinnie took the four of us to MacDonald's, and Aunt Alice took Bitsy and Mikie to Burger King because Bitsy doesn't like MacDonald's fries.

On the way home from lunch, we stopped at the video store.

This was the tricky part—getting the video we wanted without Uncle Vinnie knowing which one it was.

Watching the video wouldn't be hard because we had already worked that out. We have two VCRs, and Dad had moved one TV and VCR into our room the day before. We had told them we needed it because we wanted one night with just us big kids alone, without the little ones bothering us. And they had agreed.

But how were we going to get the video past Uncle Vinnie? Also, how were we going to get it past the clerk?

I've noticed, though, that if you get the young clerks, they don't seem to care if you have an R video or not. It's just the manager, the old guy, who won't let you get one without your parents there.

Anyway, when we got to the store, we found that our luck was holding.

Uncle Vinnie waited in the car just like Dad had done!

Yay!

And the store manager was nowhere to be seen, and when we brought *Nightmare on Elm Street* to the clerk, he just punched our card and let us go.

I grinned at Amy and she grinned back.

There was also another one Meghann and I wanted, *Teenage Models,* but Amy made a face when I picked it up, so I just said forget it.

At home, we stashed our video in my dresser drawer, under my underwear, and went back downstairs to get dressed for ice-skating.

Meghann was going to borrow Mom's old ice skates, and Marcie had a pair I had outgrown last year. They were a little tight for her, but they'd do. We weren't going on the church pond but on the one right across the street—and prayed that the boys would be tired of skating and we could have some space to ourselves.

As I stood looking out the kitchen window, I could

see that it had begun to snow. The wind was also blowing hard, swirling the snow so you could hardly see to the pond across the street. It would be great skating in the snow, like Hans Brinker or something.

I pulled on my ski jacket and hat.

"Do you really want to go out?" Meghann asked, standing beside me and looking out the window. "I'm still freezing from this morning."

"Me too," Marcie said.

"Yeah," I said. "But you'll warm up as soon as you start skating. Just like at Rockefeller Center."

"But I still can't feel my toes," Marcie said.

"They'll warm up!" I said again.

"On ice?" Marcie answered.

"I know!" Amy said. "Why don't we stay in and watch the video this afternoon? I'm cold too."

"No way!" I said. "We have to watch that at night! It's no good in daytime. Besides, then what would we watch tonight? You wouldn't let us get the other video!"

"I didn't stop you!" Amy said.

"Ha!" I said.

She shrugged. "I didn't," she said.

"We could play games tonight," Meghann said. "Or watch the video again!"

But I didn't want to watch the video now! I wanted to watch the video at night, when it was best and scariest. I wanted to skate now.

But all three of them were standing there staring at

me, lined up against me. Amy had already taken her jacket off. Three against one.

"I know how to settle it," Meghann said. "I'm president of the Cousins' Club. I say we take a vote."

"Oh, right!" I said, folding my arms and turning to stare out the window again at the snow. "Then I've already lost."

"Probably," Marcie said, laughing.

"Not if it's a tie," Amy said.

"How can it be a tie?" Meghann said.

I turned around and looked at Amy. She was grinning at me.

"No fair!" Meghann said. "You two always side with each other."

Well, sometimes.

Aunt Alice came into the kitchen then, Mikie and Bitsy trailing behind her.

Both the little kids were wearing king hats from Burger King, Bitsy's hanging over one eye.

Amy reached out and straightened it for her, but Bitsy frowned at Amy, pushed Amy's hand away, and tipped her crown sideways again.

Bitsy does have style!

Aunt Alice was carrying a stack of paper and a box of supplies, and she sat down at the kitchen table with the kids, switching on the little radio as she did.

Mom always keeps the radio there, tuned to news. Totally boring.

"I want to catch the weather forecast," Aunt Alice

said. "I heard on the car radio that we may be getting a big storm."

"Yay!" I said. "Maybe it will snow clear through to Tuesday."

"Want to do glitter painting?" Aunt Alice said, smiling up at us. "Bitsy and Mikie are going to make glitter cards for your mom and dad for when they get home."

"I'm making a birthday card for Mommy," Bitsy said.

"It's not Mom's birthday!" I said.

"And I'm making her a get-well card," Mikie said.

Mikie always has sickness on his mind. When he builds with his Legos, he's always building hospitals.

"Mom's not sick either!" I said.

"You girls going out in the snow again?" Aunt Alice asked.

"No," Meghann and Marcie said together.

"Yes," I said.

"It's awfully cold," Aunt Alice said. "I don't want you to get frostbite."

"We won't get frostbite!" I said. "Come on, Meghann, Marcie! Let's go. Skating is such fun. Isn't it, Amy?"

But neither Marcie nor Meghann looked at all like they thought skating was fun. They had both plopped down at the kitchen table, and Amy was inching toward the table too.

"I'm cold, Jen!" Meghann said. "Please, don't be mad!"

I looked over at Amy, and she shrugged.

I pulled off my mittens and my jacket and dropped them on the windowseat.

"Chickens!" I muttered.

I folded my arms. And this was supposed to be a fun day! And they were acting like big babies.

Sissies. All of them.

"Hush! Listen to this!" Aunt Alice said.

She leaned in closer to the radio and turned it up a bit.

We were all quiet then as the weather person came on. A big storm system was moving in, he said, traveling up the coast, and meeting up with this huge cold front in the North, moving down from Canada bringing heavy snows ... blah, blah, blah.

But if it was really a huge storm, then maybe Meghann and Marcie would have to stay longer. And maybe even school wouldn't open on Monday.

That could be really cool.

"Maybe you'll be snowed in here!" I said to Meghann.

She held up crossed fingers.

We all started talking then. And then we got perfectly silly and decided to make glitter cards ourselves.

The radio was still going in the background, something about airports being shut down.

"Listen to that!" I said. "Maybe Mom and Dad won't get home either. Maybe they'll get snowed in up there."

"If they got there," Aunt Alice said, kind of worried-sounding. "If this storm is coming from both south and north . . ." She sighed. "I hope they don't get stuck at an airport somewhere."

I hoped they didn't either.

But it would be kind of fun to have them gone for a few extra days—especially since that would mean that Meghann and Marcie would have to stay longer.

I took a big square of paper and folded it over to make a card—for whom? Dad? Yeah.

A welcome-home card.

I slathered it with glue, then shook out the sprinkles.

I hadn't made sprinkle cards since I was about three, I think.

I got the outer part completely covered with silver and pink sprinkles.

Great! Except that there were more sprinkles on the table than on the card, practically.

Then when the outer part was finished, I opened the card and picked up a magic marker. What should I write?

Welcome home, Dad. I've missed you.

I love you.

Nah. Too mushy. I mean, I did—I do—love him and miss him. But this should be more silly, more creative or something.

How about . . .

Roses are red, violets are blue,
When you're gone
We play with glue.
(And glitter.)

Yeah!
Or then I thought up another one:

Noses are red, toesies are blue
It's too cold to go out
And we've all got the flu.

"Listen to this!" I said.

I read my poems aloud and everyone laughed, even Bitsy.

But Mikie said, "There is no such word as 'toesies.' "

"I know, Mikie!" I said.

I made a second card then for Mom, using the "toesies" poem for hers. But then I got bored with this, although the others were still really into it.

I got up and looked out the window at the snow, then headed for the living room, where I could hear the TV. Maybe I could entice Uncle Vinnie into a game. He's really good at making up fun games. He's also good at the piano, and sometimes he just sits there making up weird songs for us all to sing.

"Uncle Vinnie?" I yelled from the hall.

No answer.

I went into the living room.

He was there, standing by the TV, his back to me. But he didn't answer me, not even when I spoke to him again.

"Uncle Vinnie?" I said.

He turned to me then. Turned to me, and I saw that he was absolutely white. I mean, there was no color in his face at all, not even in his lips.

"What?" I said. "Are you sick?"

He just stared at me as though he wasn't even seeing me.

"Are you all right?" I said again.

In the silence, I could hear the TV voice, something about airports being shut down and ...

Uncle Vinnie reached out and switched off the TV.

Then he came and put a hand on my arm, sort of leading me—no, pulling me—away from the TV and out of the living room.

"What's the matter?" I said. "What is it?"

He shook his head. He opened his mouth, as if he was going to say something to me, but no words came out.

He coughed, then cleared his throat.

"Come on out into the kitchen," he said quietly, and he didn't let go of my arm.

Something about what he was doing, the way he was acting, was scaring me.

He was really scaring me.

"Uncle Vinnie?" I said.

He just shook his head, holding my arm so tight it hurt.

We both went into the kitchen, him still holding my arm.

I pulled free and he let me go.

"Alice?" he said when we got into the kitchen.

Aunt Alice looked up at him.

Then she jumped up and came around the table.

"What?" she said.

He took her arm and took her away from the table, over toward the window.

All of us—every single one of us, even the little kids—we all got absolutely silent.

Something was wrong. Something was very, very wrong.

CHAPTER
13

A plane crash. An accident. But what plane? What flight? Nobody knew.

All we knew was that a plane had run into a hillside. A plane trying to land during a snowstorm at an airport in Vermont. . . .

It probably didn't take Aunt Alice and Uncle Vinnie all that long to tell us that that's what Uncle Vinnie had heard on the TV, but it felt like forever. And I knew, even before they did tell us, that the reason they were standing there whispering by the window for so long was because they were trying to decide whether to tell us the truth or to lie.

They told us the truth.

"Is it Mom?" I said. "Dad? Their plane?"

Aunt Alice shook her head hard. "No," she said.

"No, probably not. There are hundreds of planes on any one day, and chances are . . ."

But she didn't finish what she was saying. And she was as white as Uncle Vinnie had been.

Uncle Vinnie was already on the phone, calling the airport, he said, checking what flight it was that had . . .

Had . . .

I couldn't even think the word.

After just a minute, he put the phone down and turned to us. "Busy!" he muttered.

I looked at Amy and she looked at me.

Both of us looked at Bitsy.

She and Mikie seemed totally unconcerned—or maybe it was that they didn't understand.

They were both busy streaking glue across their pages again.

Marcie and Meghann had moved closer to each other, and they looked near tears.

"Try again!" I said, nodding toward the phone.

Uncle Vinnie picked up the phone and dialed, and even from across the room, I could clearly hear the nagging sound of the busy signal.

"We're not going to panic," Aunt Alice said as Uncle Vinnie put down the phone. "There are hundreds of planes in and out of Vermont airports on any one day."

"We wouldn't even have told you except you walked in in the middle of that bulletin," Uncle Vinnie said, looking at me—angrily, I thought, like it was my fault I had come into the living room at just that moment, although actually I hadn't heard the bulletin.

Then, like he knew what I was thinking, he came to me and held me close for a moment. "It's just that there's no sense worrying about something that probably hasn't happened," he said.

I pulled away from him.

"Call them!" I said.

"Call them?" he repeated.

"The inn!" I said. "The number's on the refrigerator. Call and see if they've—you know—checked in or something."

He and Aunt Alice exchanged looks.

Amy came and stood beside me, slipping her hand into mine.

Aunt Alice went to the phone. "I'll do it," she said. "But don't jump to conclusions. Even if they're not there yet, it could be that they're having trouble with the snow. They were picking up a rental car at the airport, and that would be hard in this much snow...."

"So if they're not there, that doesn't mean anything," Uncle Vinnie said, looking at Amy and then at me. "Remember, there's a big storm that just swept in. It could have delayed everything. Maybe they haven't even taken off yet. They might still be at the airport here in Hartford. We won't know anything till we hear what plane it was. All right?"

He was staring hard at Amy and me, like he was trying to make a bargain with us.

A not-to-worry bargain.

Like I could do that.

We stood there while Aunt Alice dialed the phone, listened as even from across the room we could hear the phone ringing, way up there in Vermont.

Listened as Aunt Alice asked if Mr. and Mrs. McDermott had checked in.

And we didn't need to be able to hear the words on the other end to know that they hadn't. All you had to do was see the look on Aunt Alice's face.

Aunt Alice asked a bunch more questions then, things about the weather and the storm and all that, and then she came right out and asked about the plane crash.

While Amy and I held each other's hands tight.

"No?" she said. "No? Then you haven't heard anything?"

I thought I could see some of the tension go out of her face.

"Well," she said. "Have them call when they get there. Yes, yes, everything's fine."

She hung up and turned to us. "They're not there yet, but the person at the desk hadn't heard anything about a plane crash. So maybe it's not even in that . . . vicinity. That town."

Maybe.

Amy and I were still holding hands.

"Still," Uncle Vinnie said, looking at his watch, "they should have been there long ago. The entire state of Vermont isn't all that big."

And he had just told us not to worry!

I looked at Amy and she looked at me.

Just us, and we'd have to take care of Bitsy.

I looked at Bitsy now. She was still slathering glue over her papers and sprinkling on sparkles like nothing had happened. Mikie too.

Could it be that she had no idea what was happening? She's smart.

I looked back at Amy.

She has enormous eyes, but now they were even bigger. Wide-eyed, holding back tears.

"Amy," I whispered. "Let's go upstairs."

She nodded.

"We're going to our room," I said, to no one in particular.

We headed for the stairs, and behind us I heard Aunt Alice say, "Girls, I think it's better for us all to stay together."

"We'll be back," I said.

Amy and I went up to our room and closed the door after us.

I sat on my bed, and Amy went across the room and sat on hers.

Weird. We always sit on the same bed.

But I understood.

"Amy?" I said.

"What?" she said back.

"What do you think?"

She shook her head. "I don't know. What do you think?"

Mom and Dad were dead. Their plane had crashed.

But it couldn't be. It didn't feel like they were dead.

If your parents were dead, wouldn't you *know* it, somehow? Wouldn't you sense it or feel it or something?

"It couldn't be their plane," Amy said.

"I know," I said.

"But what if it is?" Amy said.

"It's not," I said.

I could feel something in my throat, like a lump that wouldn't go down, or like something was tied tight around my throat.

I looked at the clock. Two-ten.

What time had the plane crashed?

If it was just before—when the news bulletin had come on TV—then it couldn't have been their plane.

Theirs was at six this morning!

I told Amy that, and she nodded. "I know," she said. "I thought that too. But they didn't say what time it crashed, did they?"

I shook my head. "No. At least I didn't hear. And Uncle Vinnie must not have heard or he wouldn't have been so upset."

But then I had another thought: Maybe he had heard. Maybe *that's* why he was so upset.

"Amy?" I said. "What should we do?"

She didn't answer.

Mom and Dad. And Mom had looked so teary last night.

"It's hard to leave your children," she had said.

Had she thought that when the plane crashed?

It hadn't crashed.

I jumped up, crossed the room, and sat on Amy's bed.

She moved over and made room for me.

"Uncle Vinnie said it's silly to worry yet," Amy said.

She picked a thread out of the quilt, then wound it 'round her finger, 'round and 'round.

"I know," I said.

"Maybe he's gotten the airport by now," she said.

I nodded.

Both of us got up and went downstairs.

Uncle Vinnie was on the phone—not speaking, tapping his fingers on the counter, annoyed like, as if he were on hold—and Aunt Alice was making coffee, and Mikie and Bitsy were still doing sprinkle cards. And Meghann and Marcie were nowhere to be seen.

"Amy!" Aunt Alice said, turning from the stove. "Jennifer! I'm glad you came down. It's really going to be all right."

She got out coffee cups and put them on the table. "Do you want anything? Hot chocolate?"

I shook my head, and Amy did too.

I felt so miserable.

"Did he hear anything?" I asked, nodding toward Uncle Vinnie and the phone.

"Not yet," Aunt Alice said.

I looked at the clock. Two-fifteen.

Just fifteen minutes ago that we had heard this?

Amy went and stood at the window, looking out, and I sat down at the table.

"Did you hear anything?" I asked Aunt Alice. "What time it happened or anything?"

She shook her head. "Your uncle is trying American Express now. They made the arrangements, the flights. But he's on hold there too. It seems the whole world is trying to find out . . ."

Her voice trailed off.

Is trying to find out if their mom and dad were on that plane?

I looked at Aunt Alice, then at Uncle Vinnie.

Their brother and sister?

Mom and Aunt Alice were sisters. Dad and Uncle Vinnie were brothers.

I looked at Amy.

What would it feel like if something happened to Amy?

Could it be worse than what I felt now?

"Aunt Alice?" I said. "If they were on that plane . . ."

"They weren't!" she said, fierce-like.

"If they were," I went on. "Did everybody . . . you know . . . did they all die?"

She sighed. "We don't even know that."

She sat down, poured coffee, then began turning her cup 'round and 'round. "We turned on the news channel a moment ago—the TV news—but we can't even get that in clearly. This snow is already interfering with the wires, I guess, even here."

So we might really get snowed in. A blizzard.

But what if it was snowing hard in Vermont? And what if Mom and Dad were in that accident but had lived? And what if they were lying there in the wreckage, and snow was coming down on them? And what if . . .

I jumped up and joined Amy at the window.

Behind me, Uncle Vinnie slammed down the phone.

"One more electronic message," he said, "and I'll tell them . . ."

And then he said a swear word, the first I had ever heard him say.

I turned around.

Aunt Alice didn't even look shocked.

Mom would have, though.

So would Dad.

We don't say bad words in our house. Don't do bad things.

We trust each other, Mom and Dad are always saying.

Could I trust them now to not be dead?

CHAPTER 14

For the rest of the afternoon, the storm continued to swirl around outside our windows, making the world white outside, sending whistling gusts of wind to cry inside the chimney.

Marcie and Meghann barely said anything to Amy and me—not mean-like, but as if they were grown-ups, being very polite.

The day just dragged on, hours that crept by like years, and still we didn't know anything—not what plane, not where Mom and Dad were. Not anything.

Both Aunt Alice and Uncle Vinnie attempted about a hundred phone calls that afternoon, but there was no answer anywhere. Uncle Vinnie kept getting a busy signal, and when he did get through to the airports, all he got was that on-hold thing.

Then, later in the afternoon, we couldn't even get that. Uncle Vinnie picked up the phone once and it was dead—absolutely dead.

"The wires are down," he said.

And then the lights began flickering, so he and Aunt Alice collected candles and Amy and I found the candle holders, and then we had an early supper because Aunt Alice was afraid we wouldn't have power for cooking later.

Not that it mattered—the dinner, that is. Our plan had been to order in pizza, but there was no way a pizza person could drive in this storm—even if we could have gotten someone on the phone. Which we couldn't.

It didn't matter. Because neither Amy nor I ate anything.

Bitsy, though, she ate like a little pig. I had a feeling, though, that she knew what was happening, because she was very quiet and very good—for her.

Amy and I were good to her too. I read her a couple of stories and Amy read her a couple, although I couldn't bring myself to read the scary Bible stories she loved.

She never asked about Mom and Dad. We had talked about it right in front of her, but she had seemed to accept all the reassurances that Mom and Dad were really all right.

Seemed to. But I wondered.

After I read her another favorite story, the one

about the anteater who only liked black ants, not red ones, she lay on my lap, her finger in her mouth, sucking noisily and rubbing her hair the way she used to do when she was little.

She was worried too.

I patted her curls and tried not to cry.

Then, when she fell asleep in my lap, Aunt Alice carried her upstairs to bed, and that's when Amy and I went up too.

It was only eight o'clock, but we went to bed.

Aunt Alice promised to wake us up when they heard something—anything.

"Even anything . . .? You know," I said.

"Anything!" she said, firmly.

So Amy and I got undressed and into pajamas and then lay down in the dark, in the same bed, both of us wide awake.

I looked at the bedside clock.

Eight-oh-four.

Where were Mom and Dad now?

Probably snug at their inn, but they hadn't been able to call because our phone line was down. And I bet they hadn't even heard about the plane crash, so they couldn't know we were worried and . . .

And maybe they weren't at the inn. Maybe they had been in that plane when it ran into the mountain in the snow.

And Dad . . . Dad who patted me and said "I know, I know." He didn't know! He'd never know how I felt now.

And then I had another thought, a dumb, weird thought, one that totally terrified me.

I thought I knew why this had happened: It was all my fault.

It was my fault because I didn't take good enough care of Mom and Dad. I mean, there was that whole thing about trust.... They trusted us ... and I broke that trust. I went out on the pond, snuck out in the night....

So they broke their part of the trust, the part where they say they'll care for us, be there for us....

They didn't mean to. I knew that.

But this was all my fault.

And even though I knew that was ridiculous, I could feel the tears coming and I blinked them back. If I started crying, I might not be able to stop.

"Jennifer?" Amy whispered.

"What?" I said.

"Do you think they're dead?"

"No," I said, even though I had no idea. "Do you?"

"I don't know," she said. "But doesn't it seem like you *should* know? I mean, if your parents are dead— wouldn't you *feel* different or something?"

I had thought that this afternoon, but still, I couldn't answer that. I sure felt different.

"Know what?" Amy said.

"What?" I answered.

"We could have kept Mom and Dad here. We could have pretended to be sick."

"Yeah?" I said.

"Yeah," she said.

"That doesn't mean it's our fault," I said.

"I didn't say it was," she said.

I heard her breath start coming in little huffy sounds, like the shaky sound that comes at the end of a big cry—or at the beginning.

"It's not our fault, Amy!" I said.

"I know!" she said.

But by then she was totally sobbing. "I want them home!"

"I do too, Amy," I said.

She sat up. The light came in from outside, the snow coming down so thickly that it brought light inside the room. I could see Amy scrubbing at her eyes.

I sat up too, got a box of tissues from my bedside table, and handed it to her.

She took a handful, buried her face in them.

For a long time she sat that way while I waited.

I needed to cry too. But I couldn't—not yet.

When she finally took the tissues away from her face, I said, "Do you need a lizard?"

She drew a big shaky breath. "Unh-uh," she said. "I need my mommy!"

The way she said it, I knew she meant to be funny— well, not funny, but like she was pretending to be a baby, like Bitsy. But it wasn't at all funny.

I needed my mommy too. And my daddy.

"And this was supposed to be our perfect day!" she said.

I had completely forgotten that. Since two o'clock, I had not thought of that even once.

"Know what?" I said. "If they call before midnight—it will be the most perfect day ever."

"*If* they call," she said. "And the phones start working and . . ."

"Yeah," I said.

We both lay down again. I kept looking at the clock, praying for time to pass, praying for morning.

Soon something would have to happen. We would have to find out. The storm would stop, and there would be reports on the radio, and the phone lines would be fixed, and . . .

I looked at the clock.

Eight-thirty-two.

Amy's breath was coming slowly, deeply, in little puffs, like she was exhausted and had fallen fast asleep.

"Amy?" I said softly.

No answer.

"You asleep, Amy?" I said again.

She stirred and turned over.

Asleep.

I turned and looked out the window.

The snow was still swirling ferociously, hitting the window with little scratchy sounds, as if ice was mixed now with the snow.

Who made the ice and the snow and the storms? Was it really God, or just something called Nature?

And was it right—fair—to tell God what to do?

I remember once, when Great-Grandma was sick, I asked Mom what she prayed for, and she said she prayed for "The best possible outcome."

She said that meant that maybe it wasn't for the best that Great-Grandma got better. She was in a lot of pain and confusion. Maybe God felt it was time to let her die. So Mom said we shouldn't ask for what we want, but for whatever God wants.

Did God want Mom and Dad to be all right? Did he want Amy and me—and Bitsy—to be orphans?

I knew what the best possible outcome was—but did God?

I looked at the clock.

Eight-forty-one.

Why were the clock hands moving so slowly?

And then I thought: Maybe the power is off. And then I thought something else: Dummy! The clock face is lit. How could the power be off?

But then why did it take so long for the hands to move?

I must have dozed off then, because next time I looked at the clock the hands had moved. A lot. It was ten-thirty.

Outside the window, snow was still swirling.

I sat up, wondering what I was feeling, why I was feeling sad.

And then I remembered, felt the hurt in my mind.

Mom and Dad.

It was pitch-black out, but for the light coming in from the snow. But there were sounds too—sounds throughout the house.

And then suddenly my door burst open and the light from the hall flooded in and Bitsy came flying in—flying across the room—and she landed hard in the middle of my bed, right on top of me and Amy.

"Mommy!" she cried. "Daddy. They didn't get in a plane crash. They just got lost in the snow and then they . . ."

She threw her arms around me and then pulled away and tried to make Amy sit up—Amy who was still sleeping soundly.

"Amy!" she yelled, tugging at Amy's shoulders. "It's okay. Mommy and Daddy are okay."

I looked up then and Aunt Alice was standing in the doorway, and so were Meghann and Marcie, all of them still in their daytime clothes, like they hadn't even gone to bed yet.

"They called," Aunt Alice said, and tears were streaming down her face, even though she hadn't cried all afternoon, while we were waiting to hear.

She came into the room and sat on the bed. "They called the neighbors, the pastor next door, because our phone was out. And he came across to tell us. In all this snow. They're all right. They're all all right."

Amy was sitting up groggily, but she was smiling,

and I was sitting up, and I was crying, and Bitsy snuggled herself against me.

And then Aunt Alice put her arms around us, around all three of us.

And we had a huge family hug. Not as good as Mom and Dad's hugs. But awfully, awfully good.

Perfect. An absolutely perfect day.

CHAPTER
15

Saturday was another perfect day. A wonderful day. It snowed, and we couldn't get out for pizza or even to go sledding because it was so cold, and we lost the electric power for two hours and the house got cold, and the phone lines were still down so we couldn't talk to Mom and Dad, and I had a fight with Meghann— but just a little one—and Aunt Alice and Uncle Vinnie were exhausted and Mikie was whiny—and it was an absolutely perfect day.

Why hadn't I realized all this before?

I know it's corny to say that you learn what's really important in life, but corny is sometimes true, I guess.

Amy and I were so happy, nothing could disturb us. I couldn't wait for Mom and Dad to get home. And I didn't care how late it was going to be, either. I just wanted to see them, to hug them, to have Dad hold me, to see Mom smile because she was with us again.

All that mattered was having Mom and Dad home again.

Late that night, everyone was settled down in the living room with games and stuff.

The power was back on, and the little kids had been watching TV, but they both fell asleep on the floor.

I got some bed pillows and tucked them under their heads, and we left them there, covered up with blankets—because they had insisted that they wanted to be up when Mom and Dad got home.

It was way past midnight, and we were all yawning and stuff, and I was beginning to wonder if I could really stay awake, when we heard their car in the driveway.

It made that crunchy sound that cars do on new, really cold snow.

We all raced to the doors and were outside on the porch before they were even out of the car.

I have never, never been so glad to see anyone in my life—even better than that year when I was four and the pastor next door dressed up as Santa and came to our house on Christmas Eve.

"Mom! Dad!" I yelled.

They came up on the porch. And then we began hugging. We hugged and hugged, and we all passed Mom and Dad back and forth among us like we'd never stop hugging.

We made it from the porch back into the living room, and we were still hugging.

Mom and Dad had heard about the plane crash and our worry, and everybody—I mean everybody—was crying. Happy tears.

Even Uncle Vinnie was wiping away tears.

"Are you all right?" Mom said, looking first at me, then at Amy.

I nodded. "Now I am," I said.

Amy nodded too. "It was awful," she said.

"I'm so sorry," Mom said. "When we heard about the accident, then heard you'd been trying to reach us—well, we were frantic. And we couldn't get home any earlier today because the airports were still closed."

"Thank goodness the pastor's number is on a different line from ours," Dad said. "You girls are all right now? It must have been awful for you."

"It was," I said.

"It was!" Amy said.

Dad looked at Uncle Vinnie. "And for you and Alice too," he said quietly.

They both nodded.

Then everybody started talking at once again, and the little kids woke up for about two minutes, but then they began whining and fussing, so Uncle Vinnie carried them up to bed.

Within about twenty minutes of Mom and Dad getting home, everybody was on the way to bed—everyone but Mom and Dad and Amy and me.

We sat in the living room a while, just looking at each other.

Mom and Dad were home.

"Know what?" I said.

"What?" Dad said.

"I have to tell you something."

"Okay," Dad said, smiling.

I didn't know any fancy way of saying this, so I just blurted it out. "I broke your trust," I said.

Neither of them said anything.

"I went out on the pond," I went on. "On a sled!"

"The church pond!" Mom said.

I didn't look up at her, but I nodded.

I could hear Mom draw a real shaky breath. But she didn't speak.

"You know about trust?" I said.

"We do," Dad said, emphasizing the word *we,* like it included him and Mom but not me.

Well, I didn't blame him.

"Well, see," I said. I took a deep breath. "I learned something. And I'm never going to do it again."

"I should hope not!" Mom said.

"I'll say!" Dad said.

We were all quiet for a long while. And then I said, "I'm glad you're home. I was so scared."

And then I blurted out the rest of it, the whole thing, how I thought that maybe because I had broken their trust, they had . . . well, died.

I mean, I knew it was stupid. But when you think

your parents are dead, you think some pretty weird things.

"But honey," Daddy said, "how could you think such a . . ."

"Know what?" Amy said. "I did too! I was afraid it was my fault!"

"Did you go out on the pond too?" Dad asked.

"Nooo," she said slowly. "But once . . ."

She looked at me and I nodded. "Once Jen and I pretended to be sick so you wouldn't go away because I didn't want Mrs. Bedford, and I was afraid that we should have done the same thing this time, and if we did, you wouldn't have died!"

Both Dad and Mom got up from their chairs, from where they'd been sitting, and they came to us.

They hugged us and hugged us, rocking us, murmuring all the things I already knew but that I needed to hear.

Except, I thought, maybe I didn't really need to hear it. Maybe all I really needed to know was that they were here. Here with us. Home.

And for the first time in a whole day, I felt absolutely safe again.

CHAPTER
16

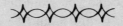

Next morning we were all standing around in the driveway, saying goodbye to Meghann and Marcie and Mikie and to Aunt Alice and Uncle Vinnie.

The snow had stopped, and although it was freezing cold, it was a beautiful day, with the sun shining on the new snow.

Amy and Marcie and Meghann and I had said long goodbyes and promised to write, and we hugged each other like anything.

I hugged Mikie too, and Bitsy hugged him fiercely.

Meghann hugged me one last time before she got into the car, and when she did, she whispered to me, "Remember my secret?"

"What one?" I said.

"You know," she said. "The one I couldn't tell?"

"Yeah?" I said back.

"I was wishing . . . well, I was wishing I was you!" she said. "Or like you."

"Like *me?*" I said.

"Hush!" she said.

She looked around, then went on quietly. "Yes, you. You're so . . . so cool or something. So sophisticated. You know just what you want and you go for it. And nothing scares you. Like that night sledding. Or that day in New York, the way you found your way back! You're cool!"

Me? She had to be kidding.

But she wasn't, I could tell.

Do I really seem like that to others? Okay on the outside, when I feel so weird on the inside?

"Thanks," I said. "But I don't feel cool. I feel weird sometimes."

"Everybody feels weird sometimes," she said. She grinned. "Like a worm. Besides, you're lucky. You've got a twin to talk to."

I looked over at Amy.

I was lucky. *Am* lucky.

And then they had to pile into the car because they had a long drive, and we all waved goodbye.

We stood there, alternately waving goodbye, then hugging our arms to ourselves to keep warm, then waving some more. Until they were out of sight.

Mom and Dad and Bitsy went back up the steps into the house, Amy and me following, and up the stairs to our rooms.

I plopped down on the bed, and Amy went straight for her lizard cage.

I watched her, thinking. So much had happened in just one week. I mean, I thought I knew a lot about growing up now, what it was and what it wasn't. What was important and what wasn't.

Like, I still didn't know what to do about boys and school and friends. And maybe I was growing up faster than Amy . . . although I wasn't so sure about that anymore. But what I did know was this: I knew what was important. I knew what made a family a family. I also knew I could make mistakes and that didn't wreck everything.

I realized something else too: There were things you couldn't do anything about, that even grown-ups couldn't do anything about.

Was that part of growing up too, realizing that? That nobody was in complete charge of life?

Anyway, it was all kind of confusing. But I guess growing up is. And I knew I'd figure it out.

I looked at Amy, cradling the lizard in her arms, like it was a big baby.

She saw me looking and smiled. "Jen?" she said. "Do you still think that everything stinks?"

"Are you kidding?" I said.

"You don't?" she said.

I shook my head.

"How come?" she said.

I shrugged.

She didn't really need me to put it into words, did she? Even if I could?

She patted the lizard's head, watching me, like waiting for an answer, and suddenly I couldn't help smiling.

Amy, my twin, right here, hugging and playing with lizards like she always did. And downstairs Mom and Dad and Bitsy, doing whatever it was they were doing. Right here, downstairs, home.

"Because," I said. "I don't think so. Some things stink. But some things . . ."

She grinned at me, and I knew that she knew exactly what I was going to say, that she felt it too.

"Some things," I said, "are positively perfect."

About the Author

PATRICIA HERMES remembers that when she was a kid the words "The cousins are coming, the cousins are coming!" meant ten or twenty extra people at the dinner table, sleeping bags overflowing the floor, and days and nights full of all sorts of adventures. It meant nonsense, noise, and even, sometimes, trouble. But most of all, it meant families together. And fun!

Ms. Hermes has taught at the grade school, junior high, and high school levels. She travels frequently throughout the country, speaking at schools and conferences to students, teachers, and parents. The mother of five children, she lives and works in New England. Among her many awards are the California Young Reader Medal, the Pine Tree Book Award, and the Hawaii Nene Award. Her books have also been named IRA/CBC Children's Choices and Notable Children's Trade Books in the field of Social Studies.